Dr

"Do

Madelaine."

Colin's face was closed and hard.

"Who's to say which of us is better off?" he asked. "I'm financially solvent and always have been. Can you say the same? What was the advantage of throwing your life away to save the family? Midge is going her own way and leaving you in the lurch. Your mother never comes near this place. What have you saved?"

"The people I love," Laine answered simply.

"Why didn't they love you enough to save you?"

Dear Reader,

Although our culture is always changing, the desire to love and be loved is a constant in every woman's heart. Silhouette Romances reflect that desire, sweeping you away with books that will make you laugh and cry, poignant stories that will move you time and time again.

This year we're featuring Romances with a playful twist. Remember those fun-loving heroines who always manage to get themselves into tricky predicaments? You'll enjoy reading about their escapades in Silhouette Romances by Brittany Young, Debbie Macomber, Annette Broadrick and Rita Rainville.

We're also publishing Romances by many of your all-time favorites such as Ginna Gray, Dixie Browning, Laurie Paige and Joan Hohl. Your overwhelming reaction to these authors has served as a touchstone for us, and we're pleased to bring you more books with Silhouette's distinctive medley of charm, wit and—above all—*romance.* I hope you enjoy this book, and the many stories to come.

Sincerely,

Rosalind Noonan
Senior Editor
SILHOUETTE BOOKS

LACEY SPRINGER

Kindred Hearts

Silhouette Romance

Published by Silhouette Books New York

America's Publisher of Contemporary Romance

SILHOUETTE BOOKS
300 E. 42nd St., New York, N.Y. 10017

Distributed by Pocket Books

ISBN: 0-373-08402-1

First Silhouette Books printing December 1985

10 9 8 7 6 5 4 3 2 1

America's Publisher of Contemporary Romance

Printed in the U.S.A.

LACEY SPRINGER

has been living a romance for the past eighteen years. Luckily, her husband is also a writer, so they share not only life and love but work, too. Settled in the Midwest, the Springer family includes four children, four cats, a dog, mice, gerbils, turtles, goldfish and garter snakes—living in appropriate habitats. At home with the Springers, visitors are always assured of one thing—plenty of fun and commotion.

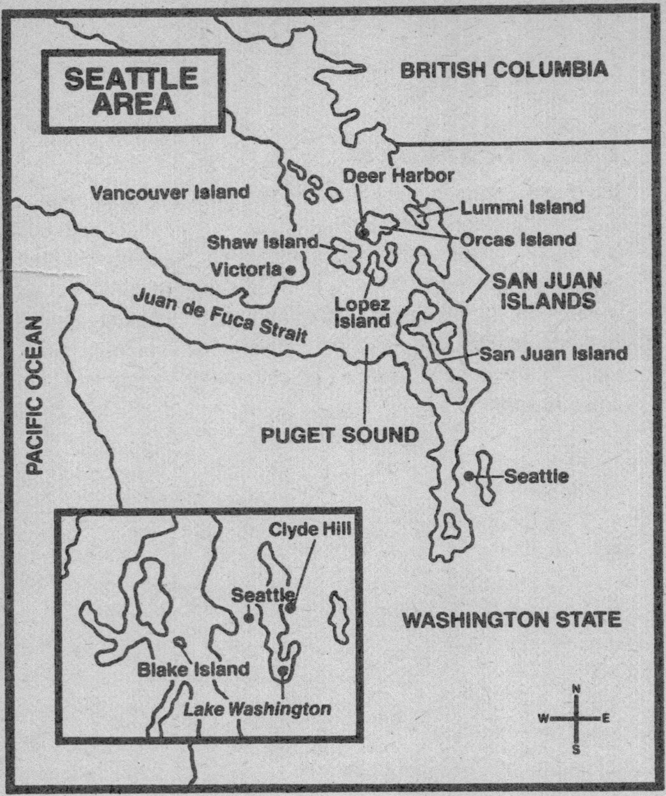
SEATTLE AREA
BRITISH COLUMBIA
Vancouver Island
Deer Harbor
Lummi Island
Shaw Island
Orcas Island
Victoria
SAN JUAN ISLANDS
Juan de Fuca Strait
Lopez Island
San Juan Island
PACIFIC OCEAN
PUGET SOUND
Seattle
Clyde Hill
Seattle
WASHINGTON STATE
Blake Island
Lake Washington
N
W
E
S

Chapter One

Andy Matheson cast a woeful look at Laine, who was stirring the shepherd's soup in a large iron pot. "I don't suppose that you'd accept my hand in marriage?"

Madelaine Morgan, called Laine by her family and friends, deftly skimmed the top of the soup with a sweep of clean white cheesecloth. "Andy, please hand me that bowl of sliced carrots."

"Does that mean no again?" Andy handed her the bowl.

Laine stirred the orange chunks into the dark-brown savory and reached for the salt once more. "What would you do if I really accepted one of your proposals, Andy? Why would you want to jeopardize a lovely friendship by marrying me?" She turned to the long, lanky man wrapped around a tall stool. "My dear, you always get romantic in January. It's the rainy season, Seattle's most depressing time. By spring you'll be delighted to be free and forget all about your January doldrums."

"You say that every year." Andy brushed ba[illegible] forelock and let his blue eyes look pathetic.

"Stop looking forlorn. There are any number of women who are dying to comfort Professor Ande- Math[illegible]lleson. Only I know that his mild exter[illegible] powerful desire to be forever fo[illegible] of golden brown You only propose to m[illegible]

Laine cro[illegible] tried to snitch one and got his fingers burned for his efforts.

"Wait until they're on the cooling racks," Laine admonished as she set the trays on the counter. She dumped the potatoes into the soup and then began turning the madeleines out of their molds. Each butter cookie fell out in a perfect shell shape.

"That's not strictly true, Laine." Andy juggled a hot cookie from hand to hand. "I think we'd be quite comfortable together. Neither of us are kids. We've gotten over the expectations of youth. We'd have a good, solid marriage."

"Speak for yourself, Andy." Laine cheerfully cut buttered toast into croutons for the soup and sprinkled them with basil and onion. "I don't feel that twenty-eight is too old to have expectations. Shame on you!"

Andy's long face took on the look of a sorrowful basset hound. "I just meant that your being a businesswoman would make you more realistic about that kind of thing."

Thoughtfully Laine piled the croutons into a plastic bowl and dusted her fingers off on her apron. "What is realistic about love? My mother and father fell in love on a ferry going over Puget Sound. No woman in my family believes love is realistic. It just is. I love you very

Chapter One

Andy Matheson cast a woeful look at Laine, who was stirring the shepherd's soup in a large iron pot. "I don't suppose that you'd accept my hand in marriage?"

Madelaine Morgan, called Laine by her family and friends, deftly skimmed the top of the soup with a sweep of clean white cheesecloth. "Andy, please hand me that bowl of sliced carrots."

"Does that mean no again?" Andy handed her the bowl.

Laine stirred the orange chunks into the dark-brown savory and reached for the salt once more. "What would you do if I really accepted one of your proposals, Andy? Why would you want to jeopardize a lovely friendship by marrying me?" She turned to the long, lanky man wrapped around a tall stool. "My dear, you always get romantic in January. It's the rainy season, Seattle's most depressing time. By spring you'll be delighted to be free and forget all about your January doldrums."

"You say that every year." Andy brushed back a blond forelock and let his blue eyes look pathetic.

"Stop looking forlorn. There are any number of women who are dying to comfort Professor Andrew Matheson. Only I know that his mild exterior masks a powerful desire to be forever footloose and fancy-free. You only propose to me because you know I'll refuse."

Laine crossed to the wall of ovens and began pulling out sheets of madeleine molds full of golden brown cookies. Andy tried to snitch one and got his fingers burned for his efforts.

"Wait until they're on the cooling racks," Laine admonished as she set the trays on the counter. She dumped the potatoes into the soup and then began turning the madeleines out of their molds. Each butter cookie fell out in a perfect shell shape.

"That's not strictly true, Laine." Andy juggled a hot cookie from hand to hand. "I think we'd be quite comfortable together. Neither of us are kids. We've gotten over the expectations of youth. We'd have a good, solid marriage."

"Speak for yourself, Andy." Laine cheerfully cut buttered toast into croutons for the soup and sprinkled them with basil and onion. "I don't feel that twenty-eight is too old to have expectations. Shame on you!"

Andy's long face took on the look of a sorrowful basset hound. "I just meant that your being a businesswoman would make you more realistic about that kind of thing."

Thoughtfully Laine piled the croutons into a plastic bowl and dusted her fingers off on her apron. "What is realistic about love? My mother and father fell in love on a ferry going over Puget Sound. No woman in my family believes love is realistic. It just is. I love you very much, Andy, but we are not in love. You know it and I know it."

A small whirlwind entered the kitchen of Maman's Restaurant. "Oh, I'm glad you're here early. I had a sudden, overwhelming croissant attack!"

Laine's twin, Mignon, threw her coat at a hook and headed toward a large pan of the delicate, flaky crescent rolls sitting on the white cupboard by the door. "My first class was canceled because the professor's houseboat was cut adrift and he couldn't get to the shore in time for class. Hello, Andy." Mignon perched on a stool next to Andy and buttered her roll.

Mignon—nicknamed Midge—was five-foot-two, as was Laine. Both had the small hands and feet of their French ancestors. Both had heart-shaped faces with deep widow's peaks. Both had fair skin and perfect mouths with curved upper lips. Their only difference was in the coloring of their eyes and hair. Mignon had the black hair and dark-brown eyes of their mother. Laine had the honey-blond hair and hazel eyes of their father. Maurice Morgan used to tease the twins about being the positive and negative of each other. In many ways it was true. Mignon was lively, enthusiastic and impulsive. Laine was quieter, more responsible and cautious.

Andy looked at his watch and grimaced. "I've got to go. I have to meet the pre-law students in half an hour. I suppose it's still raining."

"It is," Mignon nodded as Andy unfolded his six-foot-four form and morosely headed for the back door. He put on his coat, took a croissant for courage and went stoically out into the downpour.

Mignon stared at the door and sighed. "I'm sorry. Was that poor timing? Did I interrupt something?"

Laine poured some coffee and sat across from her twin at the long wooden table. "He was indulging in one of his January proposals. He was merely grateful for my refusal and an excuse to exit gracefully."

"Oh, Laine." Mignon sighed. "How long are you going to keep refusing him? What if he stops asking?"

Laine laughed. "What if he does? I like Andy very much as a friend, but I'm not interested in him as a husband."

"Really?"

"Really."

"Laine, have you thought that perhaps you're a little too particular?"

"Nope, but I've always been honest."

"I don't mean to be pushy, honey. It's just that Joe and I were so happy, even if it was for such a short time. I want you to know that happiness, too."

Laine took her sister's hand in hers and smiled into the brimming eyes. Midge's eyes would still fill with tears when thinking about Joe. They'd only been married four years before his fatal car accident. Joey, their son, had been born three months after Big Joe's death. It was typical of Midge to put Laine's happiness before her own. Laine knew from experience that it would be foolish to mention that seven years was long enough to mourn, and her sister should be looking for another man, as well. Midge steadfastly refused to entertain any thoughts of marrying again. This worried both Laine and her mother, Emilie.

"Midge, have faith. There really hasn't been time for anyone in my life. Where could I have fit him in? This is the first year we'll show a clear profit. We've finally paid off all the medical bills and family expenses. It's been a long haul, but we're making it."

"A lot of those expenses were me." Midge hung her head. "Four years of business school haven't come cheap."

"Nonsense." Laine poured some more coffee. "You're an investment. You keep our books. What would we do without you? I went to college. Why shouldn't you?"

"But so much fell on your shoulders. I wasn't good for anything after Joe's death, then dad died the same year. I know I was a zombie. After mom's heart attack I just couldn't cope with anything. All I wanted to do was to take Joey and find a cave. If it weren't for you, we wouldn't have a business at all. It's time for you to have some fun out of life, Laine. When does your turn come?"

"I like what I do, Mignon Morgan Johnson. For heaven's sake, don't make me sound like one of those long-suffering heroines out of the novels we read in high school. I'm very happy. I've wanted to own a restaurant like mom and grandmama ever since we were little. I like being good at what I do. Not everyone gets to work at what they love."

"But all you do is work," Midge wailed. "You never play!"

"Funny, I thought Joey and I were playing Sunday when we were flying that kite over on Queen Anne's Hill. I didn't feel like I was working."

"You know what I mean." Midge looked exasperated.

"I could say exactly the same to you, dear sister." Laine's expression was a mirror image of her twin's. "When do you play? If you aren't in school or working here, you're at home taking care of Joey and mom. What kind of life is that? You're no better off than I am."

"I have Joey," Midge exclaimed.

"Is he going to be an only child forever?"

Midge's face paled and she looked away. "Not fair, Laine. It's not the same." She glanced at her wristwatch. "I've got to run if I'm going to make my nine-o'clock class. See you around four to set up."

Mignon dashed out the door, pulling on her coat as she went. Laine sighed. That was the way Mignon always responded to any mention of her future. She was willing to plan Laine's future for her, but consistently refused to plan one for herself, other than that of raising her son and getting her business degree.

Laine sat alone at the table that was so old its wood had turned white from countless scrubbings. The only sounds in the kitchen were the bubbling of the soup and the ticking of the old school clock over the door to the dining room. She enjoyed this peaceful time of the day. Later the kitchen help would arrive for lunch along with the waitresses. But for now it was solely her domain. It was her thinking time. These past years she had often been too tired for thinking at night. Early in the morning she planned menus and started her stocks and sauces for lunch and dinner. This was the lull. The milkman, butcher and laundryman had delivered their loads and gone off munching croissants. This hour was entirely hers.

She considered Midge's words and the kindness behind them. Much of what her twin had said was true. Laine saw things more clearly than her sister because for the past seven years the reins had been in her hands. When her father died only five months after Joe's death, Midge had a two-month-old baby, her mother had suffered her first heart attack and the restaurant was going downhill due to transient cooks and indifferent service.

Laine had just graduated from the International School of Chefs in California. She'd received confirmation of her acceptance to work as an apprentice in Louis Dumont's Ecole de Haute Cuisine to become a Cordon Bleu, or master chef. The heritage of her grandmother and mother was about to pay off for all of them. With a Cordon Bleu at the helm, the restaurant would become a meeting place for the gourmets of the Northwest and the Morgan future would be assured.

Just when everything looked brightest, the nightmare struck. Maurice Morgan died of a stroke. The shock caused Emilie's heart attack and nearly gave Mignon a nervous breakdown following so closely on the death of her husband. It was necessary for Laine to put aside her dreams of grandeur and struggle for the survival of her family.

Maman's had always opened at 5:00 P.M. for the dinner crowd, even though it was only three blocks from the university. Laine instigated the serving of simple hot lunches to faculty and students. Like the thick shepherd's soup full of carrots, potatoes, leeks and rich gravy she was preparing today. She talked to people and found out how tired the faculty committees were of the pizza and chicken being brought in for their meetings. So Laine added carryout lunches and suppers to her menu and employed students to deliver them. Her pastries were now a byword in the area. Private homes began making arrangements for dinners and desserts from Maman's. Laine dealt with many caterers who used her foods as part of their services. She kept the traditions of the French dinner from her grandmother's day. Maman's was closed from two to five every afternoon to change from the red-and-white checkered tablecloths and flower baskets to the impeccable white linen and candles of the evening. Slowly the old clientele returned and gradually new customers were added as the reputation of her cooking and the new service spread throughout the Seattle area. Evening tables were always reserved. No one broke a reservation without a good excuse because they knew they would go on "Laine's Last List," which consisted of names who would get reservations only if a table was free after six. Currently no names were on it because no one who appreciated good food wanted to lose entrée to Maman's.

The large private dining room, which could be divided into two small rooms, was booked almost every night by some group or other. Laine concocted special treats for these parties. A child would receive a cake in the shape of his favorite cartoon character. An anniversary couple found everything trimmed in silver and white with their coffee served from grandmama's old silver set. A bride-to-be delighted over bell cookies and tiny cakes decorated in her wedding colors. To go to Maman's was to be treated as though you were a Very Important Person. Some families had been coming there for generations.

It had been a busy, exhausting, exhilarating and exciting seven years. Laine had never considered them a waste of her life. She might never become a Cordon Bleu, but she was a very fine cook and her customers never let her forget it. Her mother and sister recovered from their hurts, wrapped in the security provided by Laine's work. She felt fortunate. If marriage wasn't in her future, that was the way it would be. She couldn't bring herself to marry someone she didn't love. Affection wasn't enough. It had to be love or it would be nothing.

She dropped her chin into her hands and gazed at her cloudy reflection in the shiny surface of the stainless-steel freezer. Maybe she'd been too particular as Midge had suggested, but she'd always been honest. She knew that she was pretty because she'd had Midge around to remind her of that. There'd been a few admirers in California. There had been Andy who'd wandered in for lunch one day and become a permanent fixture. She laughed at the image of herself, her hazel eyes turning a wicked green.

"I haven't got the time to go looking for a husband." She chuckled at her own foolishness and went to stir the soup.

Friday's lunches were always hectic. The students seemed determined to have one good meal before facing a weekend of peanut butter and crackers.

Mignon came in at four to set up for supper while George O'Hara, Laine's assistant, watched over the baking chickens like a concerned nanny. George was six feet tall and five feet wide and moved around the kitchen with the grace of a ballet dancer. His broad Irish humor extended in every direction but toward his cooking. He was very serious about his vocation. His assistant, Sam Chan, was busily cutting lemons and tomatoes into tulip shapes for the garnish on Laine's Chicken Velouté. Two of Sam's nieces, Mel and Gschu, were peeling the potatoes for individual Potatoes Anna casseroles.

Laine was finishing the velouté sauce. The light-brown sauce of chicken stock, butter and flour was just beginning to thicken and would be watched closely by Sam's eagle eyes.

George pulled the sheets of miniature brioches that imitated the famous French egg bread out of the oven just as they turned a golden brown. Laine checked the potatoes in their small baking dishes and gave Mei permission to cover them with melted butter. When she removed her apron, it was George's signal that the kitchen was now his.

She went up the back stairs to the apartment living room and noticed that Mignon had already dropped off her schoolbooks and changed. She shook her head knowing that the bathroom would have every towel out of place and the soap would be lurking in some obscure corner. Mignon was incapable of leaving any article where she had originally found it.

Laine hadn't moved into the master bedroom even though her mother rarely stayed overnight. She'd always have her own room available for her use if she should visit. Emilie now preferred to live in the little house in the suburbs that Joe had bought for Mignon when he had found out that she was pregnant. Joey had friends there and green lawns to run and play on. Mignon had suggested that she and Joey move back to the apartment above the restaurant to save money, but Laine had encouraged her to keep the house for Joey's sake.

She knew that Emilie didn't visit often because the apartment had so many memories of Maurice. For the hundredth time she vowed to take some time off and redecorate the apartment so that it'd be less painful for all of them, but there had been so little opportunity.

She found the soap under the shower curtain and took a quick shower and washed her hair. She blow-dried her medium-length hair and rolled it up into a French twist. Some light makeup and a splash of cologne and she was ready to don what Mignon called her black hostess dress. Actually she had three of them. They were all similar in style and set off her one piece of good jewelry given to her by her father. It was a circle pin with a grape design of pearls. Mignon's was similar with a design of hyacinths.

In a bright royal-blue print, Mignon had just finished lighting the candles as Laine entered the dining room.

The old brass chandelier in front glowed dimly with its candle bulbs, giving a soft light to the eighty-year-old room. The high ceiling of blue created a soft shadow for the cream walls with their plaster reliefs of garlands and bows around the molding. Maman's had ceased to be a busy lunchroom and had become a charming, off the boulevard, French family restaurant.

Their first customer, as always, was Professor Rivers. He folded his umbrella, shook his hat free of raindrops, allowed Mignon to help him off with his long black coat and fixed Laine with a severe eye. "The menu on the door indicates that you're having Chicken Velouté tonight."

Laine showed the elderly man to his favorite table halfway along the wall. "That's correct, professor."

"With peas?"

"Ah, yes. But for you I've made a small casserole of candied beets. I know how you hate peas."

The older man relaxed his severe mouth. "I was afraid you might have forgotten."

Laine seated him as one of the waitresses rushed up to fill his water glass. "Professor, how could I forget anything about my best customer?"

She allowed Betty, the older waitress who worked so well with some of her elderly patrons, to soothe the professor's nerves with the brioche and tiny pats of butter in rosebud shapes. Betty and the professor would consult and consider the various salad dressings appropriate for a garden salad that was to precede his chicken.

The evening wore on with soggy people coming in from the torrent outside to be warmed by the service and food. Grouchy wet humans became civilized again in the ancient ritual of sharing food.

Laine knew many of her long-standing customers' tastes. She was ready to substitute chicken broth for the onion soup for Mrs. Markham and had George cut a chicken breast into small bits and douse it liberally with sauce for the Smith boy, whose mouth was sore from new braces. George had two teenage sons of his own and added an extra dollop of the boy's favorite cranberry sauce.

Throughout the evening she welcomed customers, commiserating with them about the weather and listening deferentially to their opinions. She admired one old couple's pictures of their grandchildren and fetched ice cream for another small guest who'd eaten so many rolls that he hadn't the room for his main course.

At nine o'clock the private party to celebrate the arrival of a visiting professor from Japan made its appearance. The celebration was capped by George entering in his spotless whites and chef's hat, assisted by Sam wheeling in a cake in the shape of Japan decorated with tiny sparklers. Laine smiled. George and Sam loved to play this kind of role. They looked so dignified and impressive as they entered, followed by the girls carrying plates and a cake cutter trimmed with ribbons matching the colors of Japan's flag.

By eleven forty-five only one young couple remained. They had finished eating an hour ago, but were still gazing deeply into each other's eyes. Mignon was watching them benevolently.

"Aren't they dear? How well I remember what that was like."

Laine shifted from foot to foot in a vain attempt to ease her sore feet, which had been encased in high heels for the past six hours. "They'd be even dearer if they'd come down to earth for a moment and pay their bill."

"Laine! That's your problem. You've no romance in your soul."

Laine thought of how she had rejected Andy just that morning for the sake of romance. "It's hard to be romantic when your feet hurt."

The couple bent toward each other with their hands entwined. The girl happened to look up and blushed in pretty confusion. She whispered to her young man and he turned to look at the room in bewilderment.

"How time flies when you're in love," Laine muttered.

The boy lurched toward them with an apologetic air and paid his bill. Mignon and Laine helped them with their coats and handed the girl her umbrella from the old marble stand by the door.

"We just got engaged," she confided to Mignon.

"Congratulations!" Mignon and Laine waved goodbye from the entryway as the couple strolled off into the night.

"Not a very romantic evening to get engaged," Laine commented.

Mignon locked the door behind them. "They won't even notice."

Laine slipped off her shoes and picked them up. Betty and Linda, the waitresses, cleaned off the lovers' table and began putting on the checkered cloths for tomorrow's lunch. Laine and Mignon went into the kitchen to eat their dinner but were detained by a concerned Sam.

"There are two strange men at the alley door who insist that Miss Mignon invited them for dinner. George is holding them at bay."

"At midnight?" Laine exclaimed.

Mignon looked confused. "I wouldn't invite someone for dinner without telling you."

Sam shook his head knowingly. "They're some kind of nuts. One even said he was Miss Mignon's teacher at the university."

"Oh, good grief!" Midge's eyes widened in consternation. "He took me up on it."

Midge rushed past Sam into the kitchen. Laine followed her sister curiously, but with a sickening sense of déjà vu. Mignon was capable of inviting almost anyone at any time to the restaurant. Most people took her good intentions for just that, but a few were more literal minded. Laine would never forget the evening a taxi driver that Midge had met showed up with his six kids. The man believed that Midge had an Italian restaurant. He'd prepared his kids for pizza and spaghetti on a night when Laine was serving Veal Braise Bougoise. Luckily one of the small party rooms was available; so Laine had seated them and quickly ordered pizza and spaghetti from a fast-food place a block over. She adjusted her rates to the fast food and the entire family had left without ever knowing the difference.

Sounds of male voices arguing with George and punctuated by Mignon's light, high voice reached her as she slipped her feet into the comfortable flats she kept in a broom closet. Sighing, she headed toward the melee to referee. George was standing protectively over Mignon with a large meat cleaver in his hand. Laine almost fell apart laughing. George was no more capable of violence than a friendly puppy. Sam had the sharper temper of the two cooks. She could feel the Chinese man moving closer to her.

"Really, George. Mr. Wasulik is my accounting instructor. It's quite all right to let him in." Mignon's eyes were dancing with glee.

A sturdy-looking man with big brown eyes sputtered, "A man who's been working all day in the rain trying to get his boat out of the middle of Lake Washington doesn't need a password, does he?"

George looked to Laine. She nodded and the large cook stepped back to allow the men to enter. Both were soaked to the skin and looked miserable in the extreme.

The shorter man with the brown eyes looked pathetically at Mignon. "You once said your sister made the greatest soup in the world. We thought it might stave off pneumonia."

Mignon turned to Laine contritely. "I did say that. Laine, this is my accounting professor, Bernard Wasulik."

Wasulik nodded, sending a spray of water in Laine's direction. "This is Colin Laird. He helped me to rescue my home, so I brought him along."

Deep-set red-brown eyes regarded Laine under sweeping eyebrows. "I can see that we've come at an inconvenient time."

"Oh no!" Midge insisted. "You come up to the apartment and get dried off a little. I'm sure Laine will find something hot for you to eat by the time you come down."

Laine tried to nod politely, wishing that she weren't so tired and knowing that there would be a mess to clean up. Mignon would give them ten towels each and completely forget about who would have to pick up after them.

The tall man with the russet eyes seemed to read her thoughts. "This is ridiculous, Bernard. These people are getting ready to close."

The shorter man waved his companion away. "We can clean up. What's a little soup between friends? Anyway, the night is young." He followed Mignon up the stairs enthusiastically.

The tall man studied Laine, who tried to keep her expression friendly. After all, she wanted Mignon to date again. She didn't want to do anything to discourage her sister. She did think that Bernard was rather inconsiderate, unlike his friend. He raised his eyebrows and with a shrug followed Bernard up the stairs.

Meanwhile, the table where the staff ate was being set by Mei. The rest of the staff had eaten around eleven when things slacked off. Usually Laine and Mignon ate alone while the staff finished setting up.

Some fresh salads magically appeared with the house dressing. Mei put a candle on the table. Laine looked bewildered. This wasn't the normal procedure. Indeed, Sam and George were busily cleaning up. It looked like an old-time movie. Everyone seemed to be running around. Betty and Linda took their leave of Laine and commented on how nice it was that the twins were going to have a romantic dinner of their own.

Laine didn't bother to set them straight. They seemed so pleased that their employers had gentlemen guests that she let them have their fun. She did stop them from putting a rose on the table.

"They only came for hot soup," she remonstrated to George.

"That's what they all say," he stated. "I know it's none of my business, Miss Madelaine, but that short one seems to be a kind of a hustler to me. He's not up to your standards, I'm thinkin'." George's brogue only came out when he was disturbed. Obviously he didn't approve of the brash Bernard. "The other one seems to be a gentleman, but I'm wondering if I shouldn't stick around, just in case."

"Don't worry, George," Laine reassured him. "No man ever took on the Morgan twins and lived to tell about it. I'll put him in our food processor and serve him as mincemeat if he gives us a hard time.

"Aw, Miss Madelaine, we all know what a softie you are. You wouldn't hurt a flea!"

The loud, raucous laugh of Bernard Wasulik blared down the stairway. Laine shuddered but held firm.

"You go on home, George. You might ask Charlie to check in an hour or so, just in case our guests decided to outstay their welcome." Charlie was the policeman who patrolled their area at night.

"That I will and gladly," George crowed, delighted that she took the problem seriously.

Mignon entered looking defensive. "Laine, he's really dreadful. I'd no idea. How are we going to get rid of him?"

"We'll feed them and show them the door," Laine said resolutely, removing the candle and turning on all the bright lights of the kitchen. Bernard trumpeted his entrance with his loud bray.

"Now that looks like a lot more than soup, doesn't it, Colin? I should have known that Maggie here would do better than just soup."

Mignon winced at the nickname Maggie but tried to be civil. Bernard sat down and began serving himself from the platter. Colin closed his eyes in disbelief briefly before he seated the two ladies himself.

Laine smiled into the eyes of the man with the clever face. How could he be a friend of the awkward Bernard? He picked up the meat platter and served her.

"Sooner begun, sooner ended." His low voice was full of sympathy. Mignon stared miserably at her plate.

So much for romance, thought Laine to herself, watching the man across from her demolish his meal. *It's men like you who remind me that there's a cruel morning light to face each day of a marriage.* She picked up her fork with equanimity.

Chapter Two

Bernard leaned back in his chair and grinned at Laine. "That was pretty good. You lay a mean table, lady. I bet you could probably do my mother's recipe for lamb stew if I gave it to you. I've been looking for a good cook for years. I just might give you the chance." He scrubbed his face with his napkin and threw it on the table.

Laine nearly choked on a sip of water but managed to keep her face straight. The man's ego was so overwhelming that it was really ridiculous. He'd practically laid across his plate, protecting it from attack with both arms. She'd been sorely tempted to assure him that no one would snatch it from him, but sternly controlled the impulse. Mignon's face was now a very bright pink. The other man handled the situation by pretending he wasn't there. Laine had the distinct feeling that she was an actor in a Theatre of the Absurd play written by a poor playwright.

"I'm glad you enjoyed the meal," Laine said dryly.

"Of course, I prefer my meat without all of that goop on it, but I understand you frogs always dump junk on your food. My mother always said a good cook never hides meat, unless he's ashamed of it."

Mignon's jaw literally dropped. Laine could recognize the battle signs in her twin's eyes. Midge was quick to love and just as quick to fight for a righteous cause. Laine's cooking was that in Midge's book. She was forestalled by the cool, deep tones of Colin Laird.

"You have to ignore my barbaric friend, Miss Morgan. His idea of a gourmet dish is a raw wiener with cold baked beans. Bernie knows when he's outclassed. He covers up his inferiority complex by trying to bring people down to his own level."

Thunderstruck, Bernard turned white and then red. He hung his head like a wounded schoolboy. "Aw, Colin."

Colin continued inexorably. "He's really a brilliant teacher and a mathematical genius, but unfortunately he has the manners and breeding of a pig. He's learned to survive, but he still lacks finesse."

Mignon looked at her accounting teacher. "Colin is right. How can you be such a great instructor and such a bore socially?"

Bernard looked like a whipped pup. "Every time someone gets to know me, they hate me."

"Well," pronounced Mignon. "You hardly endear yourself by calling people names."

"I didn't call you a name," Bernie yelped.

"Frog isn't a nice name," Mignon blasted him.

"Oh." The downcast Bernie brightened. "You can call me a Polack if you want."

"I don't want to call anyone nasty names," Mignon snapped.

"Feel free," Bernard sighed. "I knew you'd hate me outside of the classroom."

"Bernard." Laine took pity on him. "It's one o'clock in the morning. Perhaps if you called on us at a more conventional hour, we'd all be more convivial. I'm afraid it's not the best time to meet new friends."

"I thought I might catch you off guard and sort of sneak up on you." Bernard was actually addressing Mignon, who ignored him.

"Ambush is no way to make friends," Laine advised.

"It's an excellent way to make enemies," Colin seconded her.

"I'll go now," Bernard said quietly, standing up and nearly pulling the tablecloth with him. The other three grabbed the cloth in time to save the china. Glumly Bernard surveyed the damage. "It was a nice dinner."

Colin also stood up. "Say thank-you and good-night, Bernie."

Bernie straightened himself. "Thank-you and good-night."

"It was a marvelous dinner and lovely company. Forgive the conversation and our clumsiness," Colin said smoothly.

"Ditto!" Bernard agreed.

They exited silently, leaving Mignon and Laine staring at each other in shock. Suddenly they both burst out laughing. Mignon buried her face in her hands.

"I thought he'd be perfect for you, Laine. He's a wonderful teacher. He's lively, considerate and patient in the classroom. I'd no idea that out of it he'd turn into a Mr. Hyde. Oh, dear!" Tears of laughter were running down her face.

"For me! Midge, you've pulled a real boner this time. What on earth could make you think I'd be interested in a Neanderthal like him?"

"You haven't seen him teach. He's a fuzzy bear in front of a class. I feel sorry for him. How did he ever get this far without any manners?" Mignon fell into another fit of mad giggles. "I thought he was going to eat the plate!"

Laine watched her sister with pleasure. This was the first time in years she'd seen her sister fall into one of her old laughing fits. If Bernard Wasulik could make Mignon laugh, he could eat a whole set of plates and Laine would gladly provide them. She dabbed her own eyes.

"He did have a kind of offbeat charm." Her remark set them off again.

They laughed all the way up the stairs, falling into sudden attacks of glee as one or the other remembered a particularly pungent Bernard remark. Mignon always stayed overnight on Fridays. Saturday was their busiest day and it would begin early. Laine noticed when she climbed into her own bed that Mignon had fallen asleep with a smile still on her lips. She switched off the light between their twin beds and smiled in the darkness.

There was little time for laughter the next morning. Saturday meant Spaghetti Vivante. Mignon manned the tomato sauce while Laine created the thick cheese sauce that burned so easily. George arrived at nine-thirty to sauté the onions and the meat. The pasta bubbled on the stove. At precisely 9:45 the cheese and onions were mixed with the pasta and covered with the red sauce. By ten the casseroles were in the ovens and everyone turned to the mundane tasks of salad making and slicing long loaves of fresh bread.

Mignon and Laine were taking a break when a knock on the door announced the arrival of a florists's assistant with a long white box for each of the twins. Mignon's box contained a dozen red roses with a chaste white card bearing the message, "Good intentions don't excuse bad behavior. Sorry. Colin."

Laine opened her box of a dozen white roses and read the card written in a heavy black script. "Even rudeness couldn't dim your culinary genius. Forgive. Colin."

The kitchen personnel were trying hard not to stare, but their silly grins gave them away. They were congratulating themselves for their subtlety of last night. George shook his head, thinking of Bernard's ghastly personality. They'd just placed the roses into vases when the florist's boy returned. This time he hauled in two immense baskets of flowers, the kind of flowers that appear at funerals, weddings or in front of podiums in church. They stood almost as high as the twins. Panting, the boy look at them curiously.

"Are you having a party or something? The guy that sent these nearly bought out the store. He said he didn't know what you liked, so he sent a little of everything."

The fragile-looking baskets groaned under a wild display of long-stemed roses, carnations, mums, daisies, gladiolus and bird-of-paradise choked with a plethora of fern and baby's breath.

The sisters opened their cards with some misgivings. Mignon's read in the small, fine hand of a trained accountant, "I'm sorry." Laine's card said, "Your chicken is really better than lamb stew." Both were signed, "Bernie."

Laine looked at Mignon with more laughter brimming in her eyes. "You've got to give the man credit, Midge. He has his own unique style."

Mignon leaned weakly on the steel counter nearest her. "Yes, it's called overkill. Oh, dear! What are we going to do with all of this? What possessed him to put yellow gladiolus with red roses? Oh!" She leaned on the counter in a helpless paroxysm of laughter.

"We can put the roses in bud vases for the dinner tables," Laine suggested. "I suppose we could arrange some of the others in vases and put them out front."

"We'll look like a flower shop," Mignon objected.

"The lunch crowd will love it," Laine said. "I've got it! We'll give the ladies a flower as they leave to cheer them up on a January afternoon."

Actually everyone got a great deal of enjoyment from the flowers. The women who were shopping on the dreary day loved the promise of spring they took home with them. The elderly women who lived in the apartments above the street of small specialty shops were delighted with their posies. It was Mignon's duty to give away the flowers as people paid their bills. She loved giving things away, so her afternoon passed quickly.

Mei put the red and white roses in individual vases for the waitresses to set on the tables while the twins ate their lunch. George joined them.

"The chicken hash is all gone, but there's some spaghetti left." He plopped plates down in front of them. "I guess from all the flowers you didn't need Charlie's help last night." George was a terrible gossip, even if he was a loyal friend, so Laine knew when to nip potential rumors in the bud.

"They were gone before Charlie knocked," she informed him.

George cast another lure into the waters. "You didn't have any trouble with that little guy with the big mouth?"

"None at all," Laine said. "He's really a big teddy bear. He's a lot more bark than bite."

Mignon looked at her merrily. "You're mixing your metaphors, sis."

Laine ignored her. "The poor men were starved from hunting down a houseboat that had slipped its moorings on the lake. They were so tired, they probably did seem a little odd. The short one is a university professor."

"What's the other one?" George inquired.

Laine drew a blank. No one had mentioned what Colin did. She glanced at Mignon who looked equally blank. "I don't know. He was just with Professor Wasulik."

"Hmm," George snorted suspiciously.

Laine decided to steer the conversation into business channels. "Is the beef wrapped in the bacon for tonight?"

They finished their lunch talking about the beef à la mode that was on tonight's menu. It would become the Beef Hash Ménagère for Monday's lunch crowd as last night's chicken was on today's lunch menu as Chicken Capilotade. Mignon went up to change for dinner while Laine checked the dining room. She had to admit the single roses in the crystal vases added a lot to the ambience of the room. The light scent wafted across the room.

In honor of the roses Laine decided to wear a soft white wool dress that complemented her slim rounded figure. She coerced Mignon into doing her hair in French braids that coiled to a figure eight at the back. Pearl earrings shone in her small earlobes. Mignon took one look at her and changed to a soft red sheath and inserted their grandmother's garnets in her ears. Standing side by side, they looked into the mirror.

"Snow White and Rose Red," pronounced Mignon. "Remember how we loved that story as children?

Grandmama used to read it to us over and over again. We never got tired of it."

Laine hugged her sister. "I'm still not tired of it." They linked arms and lightheartedly tripped down the stairs.

Laine made a mental note to dress differently more often. The staff's amazement made her realize that she had been in a rut with the black dresses. Monday would be an easy day for her. She'd let Sam go to the market for the fresh vegetables and treat herself to a shopping spree. Mignon was far better about keeping up appearances than she was. The students at the university kept her more aware of fashions and trends. Laine didn't want to be stuffy at twenty-eight.

She reviewed the reservation list and noted that Professor Rivers was bringing two guests. He often did on Saturday nights because usually a beef entrée was served that pleased his exclusively male friends.

Laine wasn't surprised to see the professor waiting at the stroke of five for the doors to open, but she nearly fainted when she realized who his guests were. Standing beside the rotund little man were Bernie and Colin. The professor didn't seem to notice her stunned expression. He introduced his guests.

"Miss Morgan, may I introduce my two colleagues to you? This is Professor Bernard Wasulik from the school of business, and Professor Colin Laird, who chairs the history department. Gentlemen, the proprietress of this establishment, Miss Madelaine Morgan."

Bernie seized her hand with a wide grin and crushed it happily. "Glad to meet you!"

The man with the red-brown eyes and hair took her hand gently and said, "How do you do, Miss Morgan. I've been assured that yours is the best dining in town."

Having no desire to embarrass the professor, Laine took her cue from the two men and pretended not to know them. "Thank you, Professor Laird. Professor Rivers has always been very kind to us."

She led them to a corner table, knowing that the professor and his guests would probably linger in conversation for most of the evening. It gave them the privacy they appreciated for their academic discussions.

Colin looked at the red roses on the table and touched it briefly. "It's real. A nice touch, don't you think, Bernie?"

Bernie crashed into a chair. "I like big flowers better, but I don't see any of them around." His soulful brown eyes searched the room.

Laine thought quickly. "What a shame, Professor Wasulik! If you had come for lunch, you'd have seen a large array of all kinds of spring flowers. Our lunch guests admired them so greatly that we took pity on them and shared them with the ladies."

Professor Rivers looked from Bernie to Laine with confusion. "Are we going to eat or discuss horticulture? If you're not interested in eating, we could go to the botanical center for our discussion."

"We're featuring beef à la mode tonight." Laine smiled at Bernie. "Its roast beef without any sauce, except its own juice."

"That's the ticket," Bernie said heartily.

Colin sent Bernie a level look. Bernie flinched and looked at Laine apologetically. "I mean, that sounds like it will be just fine, Miss Morgan. I'm looking forward to it."

Very good, Laine thought to herself, he learns fast. She kept a weather eye on the men in the corner throughout the evening. She'd just seated a lively group of young marrieds who had made their reservations months in advance. There was a good deal of friendly banter going on about waiting three months for this meal. She responded in kind.

"Let me assure you, you won't have to wait that long to be served." She looked up from the group directly into the eyes of Colin Laird. Something in his eyes made her aware of how well she looked in her white dress and sophisticated coiffure. She blushed and turned away from his cool scrutiny to another table full of women who would be going to France for the summer. Cheerfully she explained tht Concombres Marinés were just cucumbers marinated in vinegar sauce while Artichokes à la Greque were tiny young artichokes boiled in a lemon and oil sauce. With great seriousness she went down her entire menu with the inquisitive diners and complimented them on their desire to learn about the country they would be visting. In return the nice blue-haired women chirped, chuckled and ate every last crumb of the Charlotte Russes.

Later in the evening she noticed a threesome sitting rather glumly in the corner opposite Professor Rivers's table. The older couple and their daughter were first timers. Laine was concerned about the expression on the mother's face. She was a tall stern-looking woman with white hair swept up into an elaborate chignon on top of her head. The yonger woman had the same features but without the sternness. The man wore the expression all men do when they wish they were elsewhere but are trapped by circumstances. The mother was staring with extreme distate at the dish in front of her. She'd ordered Eggplant Ménagère that Laine served in shallow earthenware casseroles imported from France.

Frosty gray eyes glared at Laine as she approached. "This eggplant is soggy," the woman pronounced. "It's totally unacceptable, even for pig slop. How dare you call yourself a French restaurant."

Laine drew in a breath. This happened rarely, but it had happened before. She knew that the party had been served some time ago since the man's and younger woman's plates were virtually empty. She could feel the daughter cringe at her mother's tone. She knew that George had served the plate directly from the oven, so the tomato sauce just had time to cover the crisp vegetable. Betty would have served the party at the same time, so the dish was soggy because the woman had deliberately let it sit in the sauce without attempting to eat it.

"I'm so sorry," Laine began.

"You should be," the woman rasped. "This is an abomination! I've eaten this in France and it was nothing like this mess!"

"Ah?" Laine said. "Of course, you're used to the French eggplants. They're much smaller and hold their shape better. I can't import them, I'm afraid. I'm so sorry you're disappointed. A palate as delicate as yours deserves better. Do let me replace the dish with something else."

"I'm no longer hungry," the woman sneered. "My appetite is ruined."

Laine felt a stab of irritation at the woman's unpleasant tone, but then she looked closely at the unhappy face. She observed the dark-blue circles under the small eyes and the reddened eyelids. The forehead was incised with lines of pain or grief. Laine sensed that the woman's rage came not from the uneaten meal, but from a deep well of misery within herself. Her father had always said that hateful people hate themselves first and the world second.

Her voice reflected the compassion she felt for anyone so unhappy. "You're right to be angry. We should make it clear that we use American eggplant in our dishes, so that those who expect the French vegetable will not be disappointed. I'll do that in the future. Still, you shouldn't pay the price for my thoughtlessness. Do let me make it up to you in some way."

To Laine's distress, the flinty eyes seemed to melt in front of her. Tears filled them as the woman turned blindly away.

"John, I wish to leave now."

Swiftly Laine got their coats but refused to let the man pay for the dinner. The woman left ahead of her husband and daughter. The younger woman only had time to say thank-you quickly over her shoulder. They dashed out the door to catch up with the weeping woman.

"That was weird." Mignon stared after the trio. "Three meals on the cuff, Laine?"

"That poor woman." Laine's voice was full of sympathy.

"Poor us, if you keep giving away free meals."

"That would come under the heading of charity," Laine stated.

"Fine," Mignon sighed. "I can hardly wait to put that on the tax forms."

A man's deep voice murmured into Laine's ear. "I know that woman. I grew up with her son, Jim. He was into drugs and died of an overdose. They buried him last week."

"Good grief!" Mignon exclaimed. "I didn't recognize them. Jim Peterson. That's his family? Oh, it was terrible, Laine. Mr. Peterson is the head of a shipping company and his son was using some of his father's ships to smuggle illegal drugs. The family has practically gone into seclusion. No wonder Mrs. Peterson is a little unbalanced."

Colin Laird continued quietly. "Beatrice and Jim were quite close. They shared a love of France. Jim wanted to be an artist, but his father wanted him in the company. I think it was the French atmosphere here that set her off. It must have reminded her of her son. You handled the situation with great sensitivity."

Laine thought sadly of the woman's eyes. She turned to Colin. "You seem to know a lot about people for a history professor. I thought the chairman of a history department would be very erudite and dry."

"Are you referring to my damp appearance last night or a lack of humor in my conversation?" Colin quirked an eyebrow at her.

Laine was unable to answer since Bernie and Professor Rivers were bearing down on them. By the time they'd extricated Bernie from the potted schefflera next to the cash register and rescued him from going out the "in" door, much to the amusement of an incoming group, all possibility of further conversation with Colin ended. Laine waved goodbye to Professors Rivers and Laird who were showing Bernie out the proper door as she took the coats of the new party.

The rest of the night was anticlimactic. Laine didn't know if it was because of the Peterson trauma or the loss of those red-brown eyes following her about her duties. It was as though a light had gone out for the evening. She couldn't recapture the heightened excitement she'd felt earlier.

By midnight Laine was relishing the thought of her one free day, Sunday. While Mignon locked up, Laine carefully retrieved the roses so that they laid in a sheaf across her arm, the white on top of the red.

"You want to take these home and tell Joey they're from one of his mother's admirers?"

"Those aren't from my admirer, Madelaine." Mignon's eyes had a wicked glint. "I have a horrible feeling that my admirer leans in the direction of giant gladiolus."

"Nonsense." Laine opened the door to the kitchen to find two extra helpers scrubbing the stainless-steel sink. She looked at George questioningly. He shrugged innocently, avoiding her eyes.

"They said to put them to work, so I did."

Wrapped in the white kitchen aprons, Bernie and Colin turned from their work and bowed. Actually Colin bowed and Bernie sort of dipped.

"We kept you up late last night," Bernie explained, "so we thought we'd help you out tonight and you could quit early."

"He's a good worker," Sam whispered, "if you keep him away from the breakables."

"Your dinner is on the table, ladies," Colin announced in his best maître d' manner, putting a white towel over his arm.

Mei relieved Laine of her flowers so that she and Mignon could sit. The next hour passed with an impromptu entertainment provided by Bernie and the staff. George and Sam took great delight in giving Bernie jobs that they both assiduously avoided. Bernie scoured the grill until it gleamed while commenting on the inferior scrubbing job that had been done previously. George rewarded his comments by setting him to cleaning the plastic garbage cans they used while cooking.

Mignon finally took pity on Bernie's determined cheerfulness under fire and had the staff do their own work. They finished and left within fifteen minutes. Still wearing his white apron, Bernie sat in his chair patiently like a dutiful child.

"I mopped the floor so don't any of you spill." Colin wisked the plates from under the twins' noses and placed them in the dishwasher.

Bernie wailed, "You're washing those dirty dishes in my clean sink!"

"That, my dear Bernie," Colin said heartlessly, "is show business."

"I've got to call a taxi and head for home." Mignon yawned.

Bernie sprang out of his chair. "I'll take you home!"

Mignon shot him a look of dismay. "Do you drive like you talk?"

"He's an excellent driver. He's a skilled operater of computers, calculators or any other mechanical device," Colin assured her. "It's only people who give him problems."

"It's quite a drive," Mignon warned.

"Oh good!" Bernie said. "I'll impress you with my driving."

"Just get me home alive," Mignon said with despair as she went to get her belongings from upstairs. When she returned, Bernie, sans apron, abruptly grabbed her suitcase.

Mignon sighed. "Warn before you grab."

Laine carefully laid the red roses in Mignon's arms to take home.

Bernie sniffed. "I see you didn't keep my flowers. Colin was right. He said you were more the rose type than the garden-flower type."

Mignon studied his woeful face. "We loved your flowers, Bernie. You gave us spring in January. When you enjoy something, you like giving it away for others to appreciate, also."

"I don't," Bernie said flatly. "I like to keep what I love."

"Bernie," commanded Mignon in exasperation, "open the door and stand back so I can go through it without my legs getting broken."

"Yes, ma'am." Bernie obeyed. Mignon stepped through the open doorway.

"Good night, Laine. Good night, Colin. Bernie, forward, march! Shut the door." The door closed ever so softly on Colin and Laine's laughter.

"She'll be good for him," Colin said. "He's really a gentle, kind man who made it up from Hell's Kitchen in New York on the strength of his prodigous mind and an impressive array of aptitudes. Your sister may find that taming him might be exhausting but well worth the results."

"He makes her laugh. That I appreciate." Laine smiled.

The silence of the big kitchen closed in around them. Laine found that she was nervously pleating the tablecloth in front of her. She was at a loss as to what to do with him. He had made no effort to join his friend. He was a virtual stranger, so she couldn't invite him upstairs to her apartment at this hour. She was too curious about him to want him to leave, but she hated to entertain him in the big sterile kitchen.

Colin seemed oblivious to the circumstances. "If you offer me a cup of coffee, I promise I'll behave and silently steal away later."

"I'm sorry," Laine apologized. "I seem to have left my manners at work. My days start rather early, so I'm not too quick after midnight." She poured two cups of coffee and put them in the microwave to heat. "I haven't thanked you for the roses or the dinner service. Thank you."

"It was nothing compared to what you suffered through last night. I did want you to understand about Bernie."

Laine brought the coffee and sat down across from him. "You must have lived in Seattle most of your life to have grown up with Jim Peterson. Thank you again for telling us about Mrs. Peterson. It made me understand her behavior without being hurt by it."

His long fingers wrapped around the white cup as he smiled at her over its rim. "I think you already had a pretty good idea of her distress before I said anything. I just wanted you to know that your assessment of the situation was correct."

Laine was thinking about how well the Scottish tweed of his coat matched the mahogany of his hair and eyes and failed to realize that a silence broken only by the ticking of the clock had fallen.

"Do you like what you see?" Colin inquired. "Or are you reserving judgment?"

"I was just reprimanding myself this afternoon for becoming eccentric," she admitted. "I've gotten so used to handling groups, I've lost the knack of relating to another person on a one-to-one basis. Please excuse me. I was admiring your coat because it matches your eyes."

"Is that a compliment?"

"Sure," Laine tried not to blush but failed. "I really am not used to this kind of thing. It's been so long."

"What kind of thing?" Both eyebrows arched capriciously.

Laine dropped her eyes to her hands. "Conversing with a strange man at one o'clock in the morning."

"But I'm not strange. We've been formally introduced by Professor Rivers. You must admit, he's quite respectable."

Laine smiled. "That doesn't change the fact that it's one in the morning."

He smiled back at her and his eyes took on golden glints that fascinated Laine as she watched the transformation. The clever, aristocratic features took on a rakish look. "Let's see. You want to know who's lurking in your kitchen with you in the dangerous hours of the morning."

"It's only that we meet so oddly...."

He put down his cup and regarded her steadily. The glints in his eyes sparkled at her. "My full name is Colin Desmond Laird. I come from one of the families who settled this city. I've got a B.A. from Harvard, an M.A. from Princeton and a doctorate from Yale to prove that I'm broad-minded and educated."

"That's quite impressive." Laine was beginning to feel extremely foolish.

"I live on a houseboat next to Bernie's on Lake Washington and have a summer home in Port Townsend. Besides my salary, I have an independent income from an inheritance and publish a new book approximtely every two years. I've never been arrested and my record is completely clean as far as I know. My reputation isn't tarnished by white slavery, attempted rape or related crimes. You're perfectly safe in my company."

"I'm glad." Laine was totally humiliated by his ironic tone.

"Good. Now, are you going to behave like an adult and invite me upstairs, or do we need to continue these games?"

Chapter Three

Laine blinked and started to laugh. She simply couldn't help herself. "That might have worked in the Elizabethan period, Sir Colin. In this situation today it'll earn you an aluminum ladle wrapped around your neck by an angry maiden or, to coin a phrase, a fat lip."

He laughed with her. "Nothing ventured, nothing gained. I gather my technique needs a little polishing."

"There's a difference between light conversation and indecent proposals, Colin. Your suggestion was accompanied by a definitely lewd inflection. My father would have challenged you to a duel. I won't put temptation in your way by inviting you upstairs at this time of night, but I'll invite you to leave." Laine started to stand up but he grabbed her hand.

"I'd like to get to know you in a more conventional way, Laine, but you must admit it would be almost impossible."

"I don't see why."

"Be logical. When can a man show an interest in you? It's not easy to impress you with my manly charms as you chase about greeting your customers. Can I hold your hand over your stew while you cook all morning? Your staff shared their concern about your health and well-being with Bernie and me." He smiled wickedly. "I had the definite impression that they wanted to hold on to me at all costs, since they obviously believe I may be your last chance."

"That's utter nonsense," yelped Laine, snatching her hand away.

His long mouth formed a slow, mischievous grin. "I heard that you haven't dated seriously for several years. I was only giving you an opportunity to save yourself from drying up and floating away into a lifetime of spinsterhood."

Laine jumped to her feet and glared at him. "If that last speech was supposed to charm me, let me tell you, it's about as popular with me as the English tea tax was with the Revolutionary army in Boston!"

"I appreciate your historic allusion for my sake. I admire independent women who speak up for themselves. I also like green eyes."

"My eyes are hazel."

"They're green when you're angry."

Laine snatched his cup and plopped it in the sink, signaling the end of the evening. "I do have a boyfriend by the name of Andy."

He leaned back and stretched out his long legs unperturbedly. "Professor Andrew Matheson of the law department. A confirmed bachelor with a fondness for good food and attractive women, but he definitely lacks the desire to either cook his own food or marry the lady. You see, I do my homework."

"Leave." Laine opened the door and stood beside it with the key in her hand.

Gracefully he rose and came to stand before her. She could either look him in the eye by raising her face upward or stare stubbornly at his third shirt button. Obstinately she concentrated on the button until his long fingers tilted her chin up. His thumb softly traced the outline of her mouth. Swiftly he leaned down and kissed her, his mouth covering hers while the other arm pulled her to him. The warm command of his lips surprised Laine, who, for the first time, realized that this man was more formidable than he seemed. Her mind ordered her senses to regroup, but her emotions rebelled and responded to the kiss. He held her lightly, so she didn't even have the excuse that it was force that kept her from pulling away. When he released her, she staggered and he steadied her with his hand.

"I haven't spent all of my time studying ancient history." He grinned, picking up the key she'd dropped and handing it to her. Before she could form a reply, he was gone.

She lingered in the doorway letting the night mist cool her flaming cheeks. Why hadn't she resisted? She'd stood like a robot and let him kiss her. Her cheeks burned again. She hadn't been a robot but a willing partner. What had overcome her common sense? Was she really so lonely that any presentable man could assume she'd return his kisses? Nonsense. Andy never tried anything. But then Andy wasn't the marrying type. How much did Colin really know about her? She was interrupted by a gravelly voice.

"You all right, Miss Morgan? I saw the lights and that the door was open. Kinda late, aren't you?"

Laine recognized the friendly crab-apple face of Officer Charlie Dodd behind the glare of his flashlight. "I just saw a friend off, Charlie. I was letting the kitchen cool off a little."

"Okay. Are you going to lock up now?"

"Yes, Charlie. Thanks for checking." She closed and locked the door. Leaning against it, she ran her tongue over her lips, which were still soft and swollen from the kiss. Then she slowly climbed the stairs. Usually she was so tired on Saturday night that she automatically went to bed and fell asleep immediatley. Tonight she was eerily aware of how hollow her footsteps sounded on the old wooden treads. She entered the living room and surveyed its friendly shabbiness. When had the rug worn through in front of the old velvet sofa? She'd never noticed that the wing chair had a spring protruding like a soldier with a dagger in his back. Where had the yellow water stain in the corner of the chair come from? Laine sat on the sagging sofa and looked around her sadly. Her living room looked as though no one lived in it. She shook her head in dismay. It was true. She'd used the apartment to sleep and change clothes, but she hadn't truly lived in it. She hadn't had the time. What was the matter with her? Didn't she have a nesting instinct like other women? How could she have let the place fall into such disarray? She rose and went to put her dress away. She was grateful that she hadn't worn one of her old blacks tonight. Her newly critical eye took in the bedroom that hadn't changed since she and Mignon were in high school. Now it seemed ridiculous to her with its pink gingham ruffles and the stuffed animals from long ago carnivals and fairs.

Memories floated around her and she let them drift through her mind. Grandmama reading folk and fairy tales to two wide-eyed little girls while Mom and Dad worked downstairs. Mama kissing them good-night, smelling of aromatic scents from the kitchen. Midge and Laine hiding Christmas presents under the bed and giggling madly. Two teenage girls in pink and white net with corsages of roses making final preparations for their first prom. Mignon preparing for her wedding, dissolving into prenuptial tears. Mignon and Laine lying sleepless with Joey's tiny crib between them the night before their father's funeral.

It had all gone so quickly. The memories crowded in until she thought of the last hard years. Many of those memories were of struggle. The struggle to bring up the business to the point where the family could survive. The struggle to attract and keep good staff. The challenge of pleasing her clientele night after night. The need to keep up excellence in her own art. The only memories in the past seven years seemed to be of overcoming obstacles. She loved her mother, sister and nephew, but she realized that she wasn't as close to them as she might be. It'd been years since she'd really talked with her mother. She saw a lot of Midge, but only talked about work. Joey was seven years old and how well did she know him? She was so involved with their survival that she'd ceased to see her family as people. She'd become a loner in her business, social and personal life. No wonder that arrogant man had believed she'd be a pushover for his advances!

She'd been losing her sense of perspective and a man who barely knew her had spotted it immediately. Beginning tomorrow, she was going to make some plans to brighten up her life in areas other than cooking.

With that promise she went to conquer the mess she knew Mignon had left for her in the bathroom. It took her fifteen minutes to find the soap in the laundry hamper, but for some reason it struck her as being funny instead of irritating. She went to sleep smiling at the absentmindedness of her untidy sister and dreamed of gliding through a forest inhabited by animals with soft red fur and wise fox faces.

True to her resolutions of the night before, Laine hunted up a bright-green wool dress to wear to church. She wore a white winter raincoat over it with a green plaid lining. Another drenching rain obscured Mount Rainier from the Seattleites, but when the congregation left the church it had passed and the sun greeted them for the first time in a week.

Laine walked home with a couple who lived above the import shop next door to her. They were young and just barely making ends meet. Although their stock was excellent, they had a few years to go before they'd be out of the woods because unlike Laine, they were paying rent, and rent was very high in the village that served the university and surrounding area.

Laine had them stop in with her and gave them some of the roast beef from last night along with some of the desserts from the freezer. They were overcome with gratitude.

"I'm packing a lot of this to take to my family today," she assured them. "Two more people don't make that much difference, honestly. After all, what are neighbors for? I haven't been a very good one, I'm afraid. Please take this as the welcoming dinner I should've given you a year ago."

Joy and Frank Marshield both blushed in embarrassment. Joy dropped her eyes under her mop of short curly hair. "We thought you older residents might resent newcomers like us."

"Please don't think that." Laine dropped some rolls into Joy's box. "It's only that we're all family businesses like yours and we all work so long and hard, we never see each other. I'm always down here or upstairs. If you ever need someone, just give a yell or come on over."

Laine felt badly when she saw Frank's grateful face and the delight on Joy's diminutive features. Why hadn't she done this sooner? They'd been next door for almost a year. It was only today that she noticed them walking ahead of her, afraid to intrude on "an old resident's" privacy. She watched them enter their back door from the alley and waved cheerfully. She'd keep an eye out for them in the future.

Laine called her taxi and finished packing the family hamper. She instructed the driver to take Lake Washington Boulevard so that she could admire the soft gray blue of the lake with Mount Rainier looming, clear and snowcapped, to the south. They crossed the floating bridge and exited in Clyde Hill to take Belleview Way to Mignon's little house in that suburb.

Joey danced out to help her with the hamper. "Aunt Laine, did you remember? Did you remember?"

On his birthday Joey had visited the restaurant with Midge and had spent his entire birthday allowance at Jones's Drugstore down the street on the old-fashioned penny candy for which the store was famous. Laine had promised him last week that she'd stop at Jones's and pick out some candy for him. She indicated the pocket of her coat and let him fish out the well-known green-and-yellow striped bag. His great brown eyes lighted up with anticipation as he hugged her and scampered off to gloat over his treasure. That would take some time as Laine had gathered forty-five different pieces of candy in the bag.

"He'll never eat lunch," Mignon moaned.

"The jawbreakers are supposed to last at least four hours," Laine teased. "I got him several different kinds."

"I'll get you for that," Mignon threatened with a smile.

"You did, you creep. It took me fifteen minutes to locate the bathroom soap last night. If you do that again, I'll get Joey ten taffy sticks instead of one and let him decorate the furniture."

"Laine, you didn't get him one of those rotten, gooey messes!"

"I certainly did. Revenge is sweet."

Mignon hurried off to the kitchen, yelling for her son before he found the lethal taffy stick. Laine was free to find her mother. Emilie was in the living room working on one of her needlepoint projects. Laine admired the elegance of the silver hair in its fluffy curls on top of the small well-shaped head. Only Emilie Morgan could get away with such an archaic style because it suited the cameo quality of her profile.

She looked up and smiled at Laine who came and kissed the parchment cheek. Emilie put aside her needlework and smoothed her black dress. She'd worn black since Maurice's death and refused to alter her widow's weeds in any way, with the exception of a white lace collar for Sundays. When Emilie put down a piece of handwork, it always signaled that she wished to have a serious talk. Laine sat in the armchair facing her mother and waited. For once her mother seemed at a loss for words. Laine had a premonition of bad news. Usually her mother would cheerfully, or bravely, plunge into any subject, no matter how difficult.

Emilie began slowly. "Midge is fixing her stuffed chicken today, so she won't need our help for a while. I wanted to talk to you about her, Laine."

Laine felt a twinge of anxiety. Was something wrong with Midge or Joey?

"No, no." Emilie read Laine's face correctly and hastened to reassure her. "They're both healthy and fine. Midge will probably have a four point for the next semester, which is an excellent way to complete her education." Emilie hesitated. "My dearest Laine, we all owe you so much. How can Midge ever repay what you've done for her and Joey? She feels she owes you a great debt of gratitude."

"That's absurd!" Laine smiled warmly. "We're family."

"You gave up your dreams and hopes to become head of this family," Emilie continued. "Now it's time for your sister to take over some of the burden of running the business."

"Mama, are you afraid that I'd be jealous of having Midge come in as a full partner? Believe me, I'm looking forward to it."

"But Midge is not," stated Emilie flatly.

The blow took Laine by surprise. She stared at the small triangular face with its sad brown eyes regarding her worriedly. Emilie's delicate hands were clasped so tightly that her wedding ring cut into her fingers.

"I know that Midge would never tell you, Laine. She'd come into the business and work but hate it with all of her heart. She'd try to hide it from you because she believes that she owes you so much. She'd never hurt you. I'm telling you this because I know that you're strong enough to accept her needs. You have a talent for the business; Mignon does not. Her talents lie elsewhere. I'm asking you, for both your sakes, to free her from her obligation so she can go on to her own achievements."

Laine froze in disbelief. So much for future plans. There wasn't going to be any partnership. No one was going to relieve her of the days of pressure and work that were her past and were now, it seemed, her future. Laine didn't doubt that her mother spoke the truth. She remembered the clues that Midge had strewed about, if Laine had possessed the wit to see them. Dutifully Midge had done the books, but never had she shown a modicum of interest in the future of the business. She rejoiced in success because Laine celebrated, but never had she shown any real concern about the restaurant. She cooked well, but wasn't inspired. She loved to meet people, but tired of the same ones every weekend. All the signs were there, but Laine had simply refused to read them.

"What does Midge want to do?"

"She has been offered a job with a computer company. It's a young company, and she feels she could be an asset to it. She's extremely interested in personnel work with the individuals who work with these machines. I don't understand it at all. Who would want to work with machines or the people who work with them? She can explain it. I've told you this today because she's supposed to give them her answer by the end of next week. She's planning to turn down their offer, but she cried the night she told me her decision, Laine. I share your disappointment. I hoped, perhaps, little Joey would grow up and be a Cordon Bleu as you wanted to be, and the business would go on and on. But then, I thought, how selfish I am. Who cares if a little restaurant comes or goes? A business isn't more important than people. I knew your sense of fairness would see this. Please talk with your sister before she sacrifices her happiness."

Laine was silent, trying to gather her resources.

"My dear Laine," Emile begged. "I know it's unfair. You sacrificed for all of us, but would it help to demand the same of Midge?"

"No, mama, of course not. I'll talk to Midge before I leave today."

"I'll go make the gravy." Emilie stood and touched the top of Laine's head. "Will you talk to her now? Otherwise neither of you will enjoy your meal."

Laine sat very still, trying to absorb the news. How could the course of lives change so suddenly?

"Ha!" Midge entered the room, bringing with her the aroma of roasting chicken. "You're foiled again. I found the taffy and exchanged it for two chicken legs." She flopped on an old hassock beside Laine. "Mama said you wanted to talk to me. Did I make a mistake in the accounts?" Mignon took in Laine's expression and visibly wilted. "So Mama ratted on me. She told you about the job offer, didn't she?"

"Midge, sometimes you're a nitwit. Don't you think I've noticed your polite disinterest in the business? Why on earth would you believe I'd enjoy chaining you to the kitchen and watching you eke out a miserable existence? It's great to know my twin sister thinks I have a personality like Genghis Khan!" Laine was rather proud of her humorous tone.

Mignon burst into predictable tears with remonstrances of debts, gratitude and related feelings. Laine refused to accept the debt.

"As grandmama would say, 'Fiddlesticks or the French equivalent.'"

"But what will you do, Laine? You're working sixteen-hour days. All these years you worked so that I could get my degree. I was going to help you so that you could have some kind of life for yourself."

"Your life is your own," Laine lectured. "My life is mine. If I've mismanaged things so that my days are too long, it's up to me to fix it. I'm in the process of doing just that. You aren't going to drag me into personnel work or computers, are you? Why should you become a restauranteur if you don't want to?"

"But I didn't support the whole family like you did," Midge wailed.

"Who knows? It might be your turn in the future. What if I were in a car accident or fell into one of my hot soups? You might end up with me on your neck for the rest of our lives. I can hear Joey explaining me to his friends now. 'That's poor old Aunt Laine. She fell into her noodle soup and came out parboiled. We take care of her, you know.'"

Midge giggled through her tears. "Oh Laine! Stop it."

"I will if you will. Midge, take that job. You want it, and you'll do it well. Let me do what I do well. We'll both be happier. Believe me!"

"Honest?" Mignon sniffed.

"Honest."

Emilie peeked around the door. "Lunch is on the table, girls. Have you, ah, had your little talk, or should I keep the food warm?"

Laine rose and hauled Midge to her feet. "We're ready, mama."

"I'm afraid we've broken a lot of traditions today." Midge looked upset.

"Ah well," said Emilie philosophically, shrugging. *"On ne peut pas faire une omelette sans casser des oeufs."*

Laine and Midge looked at each other and burst out laughing while they translated aloud, "One isn't able to make an omelette without breaking eggs."

"I never could make a good omelette," Midge opined.

"Scrambled eggs are just omelettes with split personalities," Laine comforted as they went in to lunch.

By unwritten law Laine never cooked on Sundays. She and Joey took one of their long walks while Emilie and Midge cleaned up after lunch. Joey introduced Laine to his friends and new neighborhood pets. They both enjoyed themselves immensely until they reached a garage a few blocks away from home. There they found one of Joey's schoolmates in tears, clutching a small kitten in his arms.

"I couldn't get rid of this one," he wept. "My dad says if I don't find him a home, he'll take him to the ASPCA. I found places for the other five, but no one wanted this one 'cause he's so ugly and scrawny. He's the runt of the litter." Tears streamed down the child's face.

"I can't take him 'cause grandmama's allergic," Joey said sadly as he looked at Laine expectantly.

"I can't take him, Joey." Laine hastened to add. "I don't have any time for a kitten. I really don't."

"They don't take much time. All they need is some food and a box." The eyes of both boys beseeched her. "Please!"

"We could keep him in the garage until you leave," Joey brightened up. "He wouldn't have to go near grandmama. He'd keep you company, Aunt Laine."

Laine looked into her nephew's pleading eyes. Rarely did Joey ask her for anything. She looked at the sad little gray bundle. Joey bit his lip in suspense. The distress in his face convinced her. She reached out a hand for the ball of fur. The kitten was incredibly light, but two bright-blue eyes peered out of the shaggy fur at her.

"Oh, thank you!" Joey and his friend gazed at her with veneration. "You've saved his life."

A visit to the vet was going to have to replace the dress shopping Laine decided. This creature definitely needed some kind of vitamin regime. Meanwhile she made arrangements with the boys to give it some food and milk and have it ready for transport at eight that evening when she'd leave for home. All the way back to his house, Joey told her what a neat, wonderful, terrific, super aunt she was. Why was it, Laine thought to herself, that loving members of her family always involved responsibility for someone or something? They left Joey's friend in charge of the kitten until later that evening.

Laine's heart lightened as she and Joey raced the rest of the way home. When they found a crowd waiting for them at the homestretch, Laine came to a screeching halt. Before the walk she'd changed into an old pair of Mignon's slacks with a yellow sweater under her white raincoat. A mist had come up and she could hear the telltale squelch of Midge's dirty white tennies as she slowly approached the group ahead of her which included Midge, Bernie and Colin Laird.

"Hi ya, Laine!" Bernie's face was wreathed in smiles. "We've just been invited to dinner."

Laine pushed back the curly tendrils of hair around her face that had escaped from a hasty ponytail, which she'd thrown up under Joey's impatient gaze. She dug her hands into her pockets and tried to look pleasant. Her expression seemed to cause the quiet man with the bronze eyes some amusement. They were both silent as Joey told the tale of the kitten's rescue from a cruel fate. Midge threw up her hands in helplessness.

"There goes Laine rescuing another creature. You're too softhearted!"

Laine leaned on the wrought-iron railing and looked up at her sister with a wry smile. "That's a perfect example of the pot calling the kettle black. Gentlemen, you're looking at the only female in the world who bought a crooked Christmas tree because she felt sorry for it. Or I could tell them about the whole litter of mice that lived in our closet for three months because Midge couldn't bear to turn them out of her best angora sweater."

"Cut it out, Laine." Midge blushed.

Bernie gave Midge a look that could only be described as besotted and proceeded to tell Joey about the video computer that he'd brought over for him. Joey's brown eyes were so full of wonder that they took over two-thirds of his small face. He grabbed Bernie's big hand and pulled him into the house. A laughing Midge followed them. As Laine moved to go with them, long, cool fingers covered her hand, which was grasping the railing.

"Have you forgiven me for the other night?"

Laine slipped her hand out from under his. "I believe in forgiveness, but I won't let myself get into that situation again, Colin."

"What if I promise to behave in the future?"

Laine turned to face the man leaning on the railing with one arm wrapped around a decorative post. A quick retort was on her lips, until she noticed the whiteness of his knuckles on the post. Could that be anxiety in the coppery eyes? Again she had the distinct feeling that this man wasn't what he seemed. He was like an iceberg; two-thirds of him lay hidden under the surface. She was alternately intrigued by the mystery of him and frightened by the hidden depths. Yet something in her was drawn to his quality of aloneness. She had the feeling that he was an exile in the country which was her homeland. She brought her fancies under control and opened the front door.

"Friends are always welcome." She held the door open for him.

Chapter Four

The evening sped by with much hilarity due to the various video games Bernie had provided. Even Emilie tried her fine hand at attempting to save the knight from the fire-breathing dragon.

"My poor knight always gets eaten before he makes it to the castle door," mourned Emilie. "That dragon is a *monstre terrible*."

"Wait till you get to the end, *grandmère*," trilled Joey. "The knight puts the dragon in a cage."

"I thought you slew dragons with swords," Emilie said, laughing.

"I didn't think you'd approve of that kind of violence for Joey," Bernie explained. "Besides, I felt kind of sorry for the dragon. He's only doing his job. He's supposed to eat the knight! He's really a misunderstood animal. I can program the computer to kill the dragon if you want me to."

"No, Bernie." Mignon patted his arm sympathetically. "I agree. Let him live. Up with dragons and the fantasy they represent!"

"Colin says that dragons are just our racial memory of dinosaurs. They never really existed," Bernie said sadly.

"Bernard would have loved to put on fifty pounds of armor and rush off to kill a dragon for his lady." Colin smiled at his friend.

"It was a heck of a lot easier then," Bernie asserted. "Ladies appreciated a good knight in those days. You can't impress them by adding up columns of figures or by waving a computer in the air. It's hard to get their attention today."

"You have a unique way of getting attention," Midge teased. "You'd probably have tripped over your sword and accidentally pushed the princess into the dragon's mouth."

Bernie's face took on the expression of a woeful clown. Colin came to his rescue.

"Bernard would have pulled the dragon's teeth, dragged the princess to safety and spent all of his gold paying a dentist to make dentures for the poor dragon."

"Hey, you're all making fun of me." Bernie retreated to the stool beside Emilie's chair and sat down on her needlework.

Emilie rescued him with a comforting pat on the head as she removed her petit point from harm. "*Pauvre chevalier,* poor knight. Don't let these barbarians make fun of you. Sit here by me. I'll protect you."

"At last I'm appreciated." Bernie tried unsuccessfully to look put-upon. "I always did prefer older women."

"I appreciate you, Mr. Wasulik." Joey put his small hand on Bernie's shoulder. "I like dragons, too, and I'm glad you didn't let the knight kill him."

Mignon suppressed a sigh and stepped over to take Joey's hand. "Maybe we could put the computer in your room now so you can play a little before bedtime, Joey."

"Good idea." Bernie lurched to his feet and began picking up the console and computer. "We'll play some more games. I'll set one up while you get ready for bed."

Emilie went to the kitchen for coffee while Midge, Bernie and Joey made their safari to Joey's room with the equipment.

Colin was ensconced in a deep armchair with his feet resting on an old hassock. "I can see why you do so well in the restaurant business. Your family seems to specialize in making people feel welcome."

Laine leaned back on the pillows of the sofa across from him. "You should have met my father. He never met a man he didn't like. He made friends with everyone from the policeman on the beat to the laundryman's youngest child."

"His daughters have inherited his personality as well as the beauty and charm of their mother." Colin grinned at her. "The policeman on the beat stopped me last night to ask my business when I left the restaurant. I noticed that he immediately went to check with you."

"Charlie Dodd is protective of Midge and me because of his friendship with dad. Every night he and my father used to enjoy a coffee break together and swap stories. My father traded his French stories for Charlie's Irish ones."

Electronic sounds with accompanying giggles and yelps came from the direction of Joey's room. Laine smiled. "That was a nice thing for Bernie to do. I never thought of video games for a seven-year-old. I didn't realize how much Joey wanted one. He's obviously enchanted. I think he suffers from being surrounded by women all of the time."

"Bernie designed the games for Joey's age group. He's worked like a demon on them for the past few days. When Mignon asked him to dinner last night, he worked the rest of the night to get the thing ready."

"It was a kind thing to do but rather expensive."

Colin made a dismissing gesture. "Bernie's not hurting financially. He lives on his boat from choice. In case you're interested, he's more than able to support a family."

Laine's face stung from a rush of blood. "I wasn't prying."

"I know you weren't." He smiled lazily. "It's just that Bernie throws people off in the beginning so often that he rarely gets a second chance. He's a genius in his field. He has patents on quite a few inventions. The computer companies hound him to design more software. He'd be a good investment for your sister."

Laine straightened up and answered, "The Morgan women aren't looking for investments in men. They're looking for something else."

"Oh, and what is that?"

"The list would be too long to finish in one night," Laine snapped before she realized she'd fallen neatly into one of his verbal traps. "We know we aren't perfect, so we don't require perfection. We require...genuine things."

"Could you be more specific?"

"For Bernie's sake?" Laine asked innocently.

"For the sake of all men everywhere who are dying to be loved by one of the Morgan twins."

Laine laughed. "That's strange. All those men seem to be doing quite well without us."

"Only because they don't know what they're missing. Seriously, Midge could do a lot worse than Bernie. He's certainly head over heels about her."

"Midge was very much in love with Joe. It would take an exceptional man to replace him in her life."

"What was her husband like?"

Laine leaned back into the pillows and thought. "He was gentle and kind with a deep, hearty laugh. I really didn't know him all that well. I was away at college when they dated. I was always going to get to know him better, but there just wasn't time."

"I know that feeling."

"Yes, you always think there will be time to do so much and suddenly there isn't. I've been discovering that fact myself lately." Laine looked wearily at Colin. "I can see why you must have thought that I was a sitting duck for your advances. Perhaps I gave you the idea that I was looking for that kind of thing, but I really want you to know that you were reading the cues wrong. In a sense you did me a good turn. You pointed out to me how isolated I'd become."

His eyes were soft, warm chocolate, but Laine was too caught up in her explanation to notice.

"You see, I wasn't giving an invitation or playing games. I was simply too tired after the long day to comprehend your intentions. I never did get the knack of flirting. My reactions were slow and you interpreted them as being agreeable. Right?"

"Are you trying to apologize for a simple kiss?" he inquired.

"Yes." Laine tried not to feel hopelessly adolescent.

"You're right. You are isolated. You need to get out of that kitchen and into the real world. I refuse to dismiss a harmless kiss that I know both of us enjoyed. Madelaine, don't make the mistake of putting me into the same category as Bernie. He's lonely and desperately seeks to belong to someone. You could put him in his place with the remarks you just made and he'd crawl away with his tail between his legs. I'm a different man entirely. I didn't take anything that wasn't willingly given. You know that and so do I."

"You aren't lonely?" Laine thought of the moment on the porch when he'd seemed so painfully isolated.

He shook his head impatiently. "All men are alone. It's the nature of the beast."

"I can't believe that."

"You come from a close, warm family. You're extremely loyal to each other. That's obvious. Even if my parents hadn't died in a crash years ago, I'd have been alone. You'd have been, too, if it hadn't been for the deaths in your family. You, your mother, Mignon and Joey were forced together by circumstances. Think. If your father and Joe hadn't died, where would your place have been? You'd have been a doting aunt to Mignon's children and an obedient daughter to your parents. You haven't recognized how lonely you are because you've been the head of this household for years. I'll tell you why I kissed you, Laine Morgan. If you discount your beauty, it was because I recognized in you the same loneliness I know in myself. It's as simple as that."

"You were only taking pity on me?" Laine gritted.

He looked at her with irritation. "I was taking pity on both of us."

Laine's chin lifted proudly. "I don't think of myself as a charity case."

"You don't think of yourself at all. That's your problem."

The doorbell relieved Laine of the need to rebut that statement. It was Joey's friend with the kitten.

"I'll call the taxi and be on my way in a minute," she assured him.

Bernie looked visibly disappointed when Laine announced her departure. Even he knew it was proper to offer her a ride. Fortunately for him Laine refused his reluctant offer. When she returned to the living room, she found that Colin had already called a taxi.

"I have an early class tomorrow." He looked at Laine quizzically. "I'm afraid I don't have Bernie's motivation to make a late night of it."

Emilie provided Laine with a small basket lined with a soft towel for the kitten, but she couldn't even pet the animal without sneezing. Laine waved goodbye to Joey and the rest of his video team while Colin stood behind her and laughed at the adults' antics.

"I think Joey even enjoys seeing his mother and Bernie play the games," Colin joked.

They waited alone on the front porch, as Emilie's sneezes had forced her to retreat into the house. Laine gently scratched behind the tiny kitten ears and was rewarded by a loud rusty purr.

"Joey named him Shadow. I've never had a cat because of my mother's allergy. I'm not really sure what to do with one."

"You take this one to the vet immediately to see what it has to get rid of and what it needs to build it up. From the look of it, it's going to be small." Colin looked critically at the small bundle of fur. "It looks half-starved."

"I know, but listen to him purr. He's going to grow up to match that purr. Wait and see."

The taxi pulled up to the curb and Colin tucked Laine and Shadow in the back seat and climbed in beside them after giving his address to the driver. When they arrived at the rather large houseboat docked on the lake, he asked the driver to wait. Moments later he returned carrying a large sack. This time he gave Laine's address to the driver.

"These are a few supplies you'll need to get through the night. I have two purebred Burmese, so I had a few extra things on hand. When you get a purebred, you know the cat's going to turn out," he admonished. "Why don't you let me find another home for this fellow and let me get you a good cat?"

Laine put her hand protectively over the kitten. "This is the cat Joey asked me to take. This is the cat I want."

He was still looking at her oddly when they arrived. She let him follow her up the stairs to the apartment so that he could show her what to do for the kitten. After he'd explained the intricacies of the litter box and placed it in the bathroom, he introduced it to Shadow who enthusiastically demonstrated his intelligence by immediately recognizing its use. They then proceeded to the kitchen where Colin showed her how to mix cottage cheese with the cat food he had gotten from his vet. After Shadow had wolfed it down, Colin reminded Laine that a kitten should eat at least four times a day until it was three months old.

"It's like raising a baby!" Laine looked a little daunted.

"It's a better investment. He'll grow up in less than a year and be loyal to you for the rest of his life. You can't always say that about children, can you?" Colin poured fresh water into a small dish and carefully put it on the floor. They watched the kitten lap the water and then take several steps toward Laine before collapsing in a heap by her foot.

"Should I fix a place for him to sleep?" Laine inquired.

"He'll make that choice himself." Colin shrugged. "It's only nine o'clock. It's still a respectable time to offer a cup of coffee. I promise to be gone by ten."

Laine turned with flaming cheeks to make the coffee. It had been rude of her not to offer him something. After all, he'd been kind enough to provide all of the kitty supplies for the night.

Leaving her to brew coffee, he scooped up the kitten and went into the living room. She was so nervous that she dropped the spoons and put the milk in the sugar bowl.

"This is ridiculous," she reprimanded herself softly. "I'm a grown woman, capable of handling a man's presence in my home without incident...I hope." She took the tray in and found him sitting in her father's old chair with the protruding spring.

"This apartment could use a face lift."

She set the tray on the butler's table in front of the sofa. "I've been planning to redecorate. I was going to buy some paint tomorrow, but Shadow has to come first."

He accepted his cup of coffee. "With all of that dark walnut woodwork, you need some light colors. You have some good pieces; the Murphy cabinet in the kitchen, that butler's table, and the chest beside the sofa."

"That was my grandmother's wedding chest. She brought it with her from France. I'd like to do the apartment to match some of the older pieces, but I don't have time for the research." Laine noticed that the cat was now snoring lightly on Colin's shoulder. She hid a smile in her cup. "I saw a picture of a kitchen I loved with the same wooden cupboards as mine, but the walls were white-washed and had blue veinlike markings. It was all in blue and white, and absolutely oozed cheerfulness."

"You mean the French-cottage look. I've been in some. Gives you a bright, refreshing feeling." He raised his cup to avoid the kitten who was traversing his chest with tiny claws on route to his lap. "White shutters would hide the window facing the alley. That's one of the things that makes your kitchen so depressing."

"In the meantime, I do have a restaurant to keep afloat. It'll take forever to redo the apartment. And I have to consider expenses. A new coat of paint should improve it a lot."

"You always economize when it comes to yourself, don't you?"

"Pardon?" Laine's cup hit her saucer with an audible clink.

"Correct me if I'm wrong. Since your father died, you've managed the restaurant virtually alone. You've single-handedly supported your family. Bernie told me tonight that Mignon was overjoyed because she was going to accept a job with a computer company after graduation. Doesn't that leave you holding the bag?" Colin put his cup down. "I think you should at least have a pleasant place to come home to. I've just sent in a manuscript to my publisher, so I have some free time for the next few weeks. Bernie is always looking for honest work to keep his fertile mind busy. Let us help you."

Laine was overcome. "One, I'm not holding the bag as you put it. I love the restaurant business. Two, I let myself fall into this rut and it's up to me to get myself out of it. No one is to blame but me. I made the choices. Three, I can't ask that of you and Bernie. I hardly know you."

Colin rose, lifting the kitten up carefully and depositing him on the vacated chair seat. "Let me put it this way. You can accomplish three things by letting us assist you. One you'll give Bernie an excuse to see Mignon. Two, I enjoy painting and playing handyman. Three, you might find that you like having me around."

"What if none of the three work out?" Laine asked.

"You'll have a new apartment and no strings attached."

"Gratitude is a heavy chain around someone's heart." Laine shook her head.

"I know." Colin smiled. "I'm hoping to use it to weaken your resolve."

Laine gave him a bewildered look. "What?"

He touched her cheek briefly with his fingertips and his touch was as intimate as a kiss. "I'm trying to make you an offer you can't refuse. Once you're helpless with gratitude, I'll strike."

Laine blinked. "Don't you think you've weakened your plans a little by revealing them to me?"

"Let's say I believe in fair play. I'm giving myself a handicap." He stood in the doorway. "I'll do a little research and report to you tomorrow. You close at ten, so you won't be tired. Don't get up. I can let myself out. Good night, Madelaine. Did you know that your name means tower of strength?"

Laine made it to the top of the stairs as he reached the bottom. "What does Colin mean?" she called to the shadow at the foot of the stairs.

The dry, amused voice floated up to her. "Victory, of course."

His mocking chuckle filled the stairwell until the closing door cut it off. Abruptly Laine sat down on the top step. What a puzzle the man was. One moment he's telling her how inferior her cat is and the next he's allowing it to claw its way across his chest. One day he appears in her life and receives a resounding rejection, then he offers to help decorate her apartment. Just when she thinks he's under some kind of control, he issues a declaration of dishonorable intentions.

Something in his rust-colored eyes warned her not to take him too lightly. His fast exit from the apartment had stymied her refusal of his services as a decorator. Tomorrow she'd gently but firmly put him off. She didn't want to owe the man anything.

The next day the vet reported that Shadow was free of fleas but did have worms and showed signs of malnutrition. He was medicated and given a bath, making the little cat look like a fuzzy ball with blue eyes. His kitten shots added injury to insult, and by the time they left he was clinging to Laine for dear life.

Afterward, she barely made it downstairs in time to oversee lunch. George looked up from the immense pan of hash he was carrying as she entered.

"How's the new kitty?" he asked.

"How'd you know?" Laine poured a quick cup of coffee as she surveyed the kitchen. Everything was ready in spite of her playing hooky. She drew a relieved breath.

"You know," George said, walking around Sam who was stirring the chili that was a Monday through Friday staple for lunches, "we're quite capable of carrying on for a week or two without you. Your sister stopped by to ask about the kitty while you were out. Your young man was with her. They came to take measurements of the apartment for your redecorating. At least take off Monday through Thursday. You never take time for yourself. Don't you trust us after all these years?"

Tears sprung into Laine's eyes and she shook her head. "It's not that I don't trust you and Sam, George. It's only that..."

George's big hand patted her back as Sam put a warm butterfly roll beside her coffee. "I know. It's been a real hassle building up the business, and you're used to it all falling on you. That's the point. You trained us. Now you need to have faith in your teaching. You know we'll follow the menus just as we have for years. Have we ever failed you?"

"Of course not." Laine hugged the big man and touched Sam's shoulder.

"We could stagger our hours a little so that one of us could do the early preparation, and someone could be here to oversee cleanup. Why don't you take off this week and start your redecorating? It we get into trouble, you'll be right upstairs. Of course, you're welcome to be hostess. Neither Sam nor I have the good looks or disposition to charm the customers. We talked this over with Miss Mignon and your fella this morning. We all voted to do it."

Now the tears did overflow. George pulled out a gigantic handkerchief and handed it to her. Laine was so overwhelmed that she didn't even correct the assumption that Colin was her young man.

George stood over her, patting her back and making soothing sounds. After she'd washed her face and prepared to go into the dining room, Sam whispered that they'd worked out a new schedule for the help. She could look it over after the lunch crowd left. It seemed as though everything had been taken care of.

The noon crowd of students and teachers was particularly lively in gratitude for the hot food and warm welcome of Maman's on another wet January day. Laine enjoyed the bantering of the young people and their vociferous appreciation of her food. It wasn't until it was almost time to close the restaurant to prepare for dinner that she noticed the lone occupant of the corner table. Janet, one of her lunch waitresses, led her to one side.

"She came in behind that big group of drama kids. She asked me to tell you that she'd like to talk to you when you were free. I told her that you'd be busy until about two, but she said she'd wait. She's already paid her bill."

Laine recognized the girl who'd been with the Peterson woman on Saturday night. She went to sit in the chair opposite the girl. "Hi. Janet said you wanted to talk to me."

The rather long-faced girl looked at her with apologetic gray eyes. "I wanted to thank you for your kindness last Saturday. My father sent this check for the inconvenience and embarrassment we must have caused you." She ducked her head and light-brown hair fell across her face. "My mother hasn't been well since by brother died. I'm sorry that she made such a scene." She suddenly remembered her manners. "Oh, my name is Payne Peterson." She awkwardly stuck out her hand, which Laine took warmly.

"It was obvious that your mother was distressed by something more important than an eggplant. There's no need to feel badly, Payne." Laine glanced at the check and looked up at Payne with horrified eyes. "I can't possibly accept this. It's far beyond the price of the meals!"

Payne's eyes filled with tears. "Oh, please take it. If you don't, my father will bring it back himself. He'll think I'm an idiot for not giving it to you with more expertise. He thinks I'm a nitwit anyway. I realize that I've no social graces. If I were like my brother, I'd have charmed you into accepting it."

Laine studied the watering eyes and the reddening nose of the tall girl. "It looks as though the situation has been tough for you, too."

Payne mopped a tear with her napkin. "I'm sorry. I didn't come here to cry all over you." Tears were streaming down her cheeks.

Laine reached over and pulled the girl to her feet. "Come upstairs to the apartment while the girls set up for dinner. It'll be easier to talk up there." She hustled Payne, still clutching her napkin to her face, up the stairs. Mignon was on her way down. She greeted Laine and gave her a look that showed she'd taken in the situation and not to worry. Laine knew her sister would see that the set up was completed. Monday night's menu was a simple Quiche Lorraine with onion soup and thick French bread. George could handle this meal in his sleep.

She sat the weeping girl down on the old sofa and provided her with a box of tissues. After a few minutes Payne looked up with a crooked smile.

"I don't know what came over me."

"Grief over your brother," Laine suggested sympathetically.

"Partially. He was eight years older and I thought he was the greatest hero there was. It was bad enough when he died, but the way he died was so awful. You see, he was a drug addict, but we didn't know it." Payne hung her head dolefully. "It was such a shock. My mother and father thought the sun rose and set with Jim. His death nearly killed her, and my father just goes around looking like a zombie."

"They're lucky they still have you," Laine comforted her.

"Oh, they don't even know I'm there. I'm not sure they ever did. When Jim died it was as though their only child had gone. They don't seem to remember that I'm alive." Payne stopped herself in horror. "Oh, that's a terrible thing to say, even if it's true. He was the boy, you see. He was the one who would take over the business and do great things."

"I remember how grief can shut you away from people. When my sister's husband died, she didn't communicate with me for weeks and we're twins. Your parents are probably too full of pain to share it with anyone. Eventually they'll get over it. Then they'll be glad you're there."

"Do you really think so?" Payne looked wistful. "I wish I could believe that. I'm so lonely. All of my college friends have sort of drifted away. Some got married and others got jobs that took them out of town. I didn't do either, I really admire you, Laine."

"Oh, Payne. I'm trying to get myself out of a rut. Don't admire me, please."

"But I do. Look at how you run your own business and, in spite of what Mother said the other night, your food is excellent. I've been to France lots of times so I know. I think that's what really set her off. The atmosphere and the smells reminded her of France. Mother and Jim loved France." Tears started again.

"What do you like to do, Payne?" Laine asked. She thought it would help Payne to take her mind off things by thinking about getting a job.

"I like to cook. I majored in home economics with an emphasis in culinary engineering. I was going to teach or work my way up in a hotel restaurant, but mother didn't like the idea."

"Why don't you go for it, Payne? My chefs have been with me for years or I'd give you a try. My business is too small to accommodate another cook, but I'm sure there are openings in a town as large as Seattle."

"Maybe I will," Payne said thoughtfully. "You're right. Sitting here and feeling sorry for myself isn't going to make my life count for anything. It can't hurt to try, even if I am an abject coward."

"Don't put yourself down. We're all cowards about something. Look around you. See how I've let this place go downhill because I was too cowardly to change it? I've let my college friends fall by the wayside because I let myself get too busy."

Payne looked around timidly. "It is kind of dark in here."

Laine laughed. "It's awful! I know. I'm in the process of changing it. You were a home-economics major. What do you think? A neighbor of yours has volunteered to help me improve it. Do you remember Colin Laird?"

"Colin?" Payne cried. "Colin was my first great love!"

Chapter Five

Oh?" Laine carefully kept her voice neutral.

Payne smiled a lopsided smile. "He was my knight in shining armor during my grade-school years. When I was in first grade the kids discovered my middle name was Ulalie. We had to put our initials on all our belongings in school. So everything I owned was labeled P. U. Peterson."

"Oh no!"

"Oh yes! My mother's middle name was Ulalie, so my parents never considered the repercussions, but the other children made my life miserable. Jim was two years younger than Colin and really looked up to him. They never noticed me much, but one day when I was crying my heart out Colin found me. He was a junior in high school then. He dried my tears and took me out for ice cream. I told him the whole sad story. He was the first person who ever listened to me or talked to me as though I was an adult. He made me realize that my tears only encouraged the other kids to torment me. He told me to laugh when they teased and pretend not to care. It took awhile but he was right."

Payne smiled. "I always had a soft spot in my heart for Colin. He was so unfailingly kind. Even when Jim began to resent Colin, I wouldn't go along with him."

"Why would Jim resent Colin?"

"Colin did everything that Jim wanted to do. Did you know that Colin is a silent partner in my father's shipping company? Colin's father and my dad built up the company together."

"No, I knew he was a writer, but I didn't know about the company." Laine now knew the source of Colin's independent income.

"Desmond Laird was one of the wealthiest men in Seattle. Our company was only one of his interests. Anyway, Desmond expected his son to take over the business after he graduated from Harvard but Colin refused. Colin wanted to be a writer and a teacher. According to my mother, Desmond and Sylvia were never around enough to influence him. He was really raised by a series of housekeepers."

Laine was beginning to understand Colin's remark about all men being lonely. "That explains a lot about him."

"He had the courage to fight for his convictions," Payne continued. "Jim envied Colin because he couldn't face the prospect of trying to make it on his own. Desmond refused to help Colin in any way if he didn't buckle under and go to work for him. Jim couldn't bring himself to take on my father and do without what he called the good life. Colin made a success of himself. There's hardly a coffee table in Seattle that doesn't have one of Sy Desmond's books on it."

"Good grief! Is that the name he writes under?" Laine recognized the name. Who hadn't read the popular history books with the gorgeous illustrations? Many college students had passed tests because of his easy to read, humorous treatment of the past.

"He must have been pretty young when his first book was published," Laine commented.

"It was his master's thesis. The thesis committee was ready to fail him at first because they enjoyed it so much, and they didn't think it could meet academic standards. The more successful Colin became, the more embittered Jim became. I think he saw in Colin all of the things he wanted to be. He wasn't willing to pay the price for the talent or the freedom." Payne studied her hands. "It's terrible to talk about my brother like that, but it's true. I didn't realize until I was talking to you that I'm on the same path. I said I admired you and I do, but I've no right to envy you what I haven't worked for on my own. You have worked."

"It seems to me that you've got yourself together, Payne." Laine studied the girl across from her. "I wouldn't judge Jim too harshly. He took the easy way out, but found even that was too difficult for him. He certainly paid for his choice."

"But he left a lot of suffering and misery behind for the people who loved him. It was a childish and selfish choice. I'm not going to fall into the same trap."

"Good for you!"

Payne blushed. "Look at the time! I've interfered with your schedule long enough." She stood up to leave. "I'm glad you're renovating this apartment. You're much too nice a person to live in a cave."

Laine showed her to the door. "If you have some time, Payne, would you help me with the apartment? Colin is meeting me here tonight about ten to discuss it. I'd love to have your input, but I don't want to impose."

"Oh, please impose!" Payne's face lighted up with such eagerness that Laine was shamed at such a simple suggestion.

Quickly Laine outlined her ideas about a French-cottage look. "Colin will think structurally, but I need someone to advise me about how to decorate afterward."

"I'd love to meet you at ten. Let me take a look around to see what you've already got while you dress. Maybe I can work up some ideas by tonight." Payne's voice was bubbling with anticipation.

"Feel free to wander." Laine smiled at the other girl and swiftly fed Shadow who'd spent the afternoon sleeping in the bathroom sink. While she dressed, she heard kitchen cupboards being opened and closed along with the doors to the master bedroom and her grand-mother's room. She could hear Payne talking to Shadow as she investigated. Shadow contributed various merks and meows to the conversation.

When Laine came out of her room, she almost col-lided with Payne who was ... notebook ...

...ersary party. In no time at all ...clock and the night's work was over.

...ne was beginning to feel really guilty. Last night ...decided to tell Colin that she couldn't impose on ...in regard to the apartment. Then she'd promptly ...ned around and invited Payne to help her. She de-...ed that she'd have to be very firm and not let every-...e get carried away.

All of her good intentions suffered a severe setback ...hen she found an enthusiastic mob waiting in the ...itchen. Seated around the wooden table were Colin, Bernie, Payne, Andy and Mignon. George and Sam were looking over their shoulders at the papers lying on the table. Mignon looked up from a drawing with bright eyes.

"Oh, Laine. Wait until you see this?"

Laine's heart sank. Didn't they realize that there was a real financial limitation to this endeavour? She slid into a chair next to her sister and picked up some of the drawings while she tried to understand the chorus of voices all talking to her at once. The drawings were de-... children's illustrated storybook. She

ender. The bathroom at the end of the hall would have its old maroon and gray tiles replaced by black and white.

"Those old fixtures are back in now. You wouldn't believe what you'd have to pay for one of those old claw-footed bathtubs today." Payne's voice was full of enthusiasm.

Colin hadn't said a word, but Laine was intensely aware of his warm gaze. Payne was murmuring things about "St. James patterns" and "Serpentine in mauve." Even Andy got caught up in the general merriment and made suggestions. Bernie was talking about an intercom from the restaurant kitchen to the apartment. Sam mentioned that a vase he had at home would match the blue of the new kitchen perfectly. Not to be outdone, George offered some Irish linen for curtains in the study.

It took some time to get everyone's attention, but eventually Laine accomplished it. She looked at them regretfully. "I can't tell you how much I love what you've done here. It's beautiful. It's nicer than anything I've ever dreamed about."

They all beamed at her. Even Colin allowed himself a satisfied smile. That made it all the more difficult to squelch their enjoyment. "You've put in so much work, Colin, Bernie, Payne. I love it all but I simply cannot possibly afford this."

"Nonsense." Colin spoke for the first time. "I don't anticipate that we'll spend more than a couple hundred dollars for the whole thing."

"How can that be possible?" Laine tried not to be too hopeful.

"Notice that the designs deal mostly with what's in the apartment. We're just rearranging things. We change some things with paint or stain."

"I have a brother-in-law who sells bathroom and kitchen tiles," Andy volunteered. "I can get those for almost nothing."

Mignon added, "Paint isn't expensive."

"I get all of my equipment free just by designing a little something for someone," Bernie said, shrugging.

When Colin spoke the others subsided. "The shutters are residing in my storeroom in Port Townsend. They were part of a project that never got off the ground. There's no sense in letting them go to waste."

"I can't accept that expensive a gift from you or anyone," Laine stated firmly.

"All right. I'll give them to the Society for Soldiers and Sailors and we'll go down to their warehouse and buy them for a few dollars, if that will make you feel better."

"I love to hunt for old materials and bargains, Laine," Payne begged. "I haven't had this much fun in years. Please don't spoil it."

Colin turned to Midge. "Is she always this proud, or is it me?"

Midge pretended to consider. "Madelaine has always been somewhat stiff-necked about accepting help. It's not just you. She's been head of the house for so long that it's gotten to her."

"I can testify to that," George added.

"Thanks a lot, gang." Laine tried not to smile.

"Well," said Andy, sensible as always. "Why don't we work on the apartment until the money runs out? Then we'll make do with what we have."

"That's a wonderful idea," praised Payne, looking at him with admiration.

"Thanks." Andy looked distinctly smug.

Sam, Mei and Gschu nodded their heads. "It's not good for a woman to live in unhappy surroundings,"

Sam pronounced. "A pretty lady should have pretty things around her."

"All those in favor of this plan say 'aye,'" Colin rapped quickly.

Everyone shouted "aye."

"All those opposed?"

Under the pressure of nine glares, Laine said nothing.

Colin tapped the table briskly with a pencil. "Nine ayes, no nays and one abstention. The ayes have it. We'll start Thursday. That'll give us two days to gather supplies. Payne will be treasurer and keep books. Everyone will work when they can fit it in. Agreed?" Another chorus of ayes greeted him. "If there's no further business, we'll adjourn for refreshments."

"Is my mouth still hanging open?" Laine whispered to Midge.

"No, but your eyes are still a trifle glazed." Midge laughed. "Oh, just go with the flow for once, Laine. We'll all enjoy the project so much."

Laine's eyes fell on the sketch of the living room. Colin had drawn a small fluff of gray fur curled up on the sofa. "I must be coming down with something."

"What?" Midge poured Laine some coffee.

"I seem to be bawling over the least little thing. Look, Midge. He even put Shadow in the picture."

Midge looked sharply at her sister, taking in the overbright hazel eyes. "You may be coming down with something, sis, but I don't think it could be categorized as an illness."

"What?"

"Never mind. Excuse me a moment, I see that Bernie is attacking the coffee maker. Oops! Too late!" She looked wryly at the red-faced Bernie who was holding the broken spigot in his hand. "It's hard to believe he's such a genius with mechanical things. Remind me to keep him away from the paint." Midge went over to relieve Bernie of the broken spigot and to help him clean up the pool of coffee on the floor.

Payne and Andy were laughing at the sight of Midge bullying Bernie. The kitchen staff was cheerfully finishing cleanup and making humorous comments aimed at Bernie who was taking it all with equanimity. The kitchen rang with the banter of friends. The friendly symphony around her reminded her of her childhood days when her parents would entertain in their kitchen.

Laine studied the drawings on the table, discovering something innovative in every design. "You look a million miles away, Laine." Colin pulled up a chair and sat down beside her.

"I was just admiring your work. I can't tell you how much I appreciate the time you put into these." She delicately touched the drawing of the living room. "Shadow would appreciate your thoughfulness, too."

"Don't give me any thanks until the job is done. Payne should be given credit for the colors. She told me about your collection of quilts and ironstone. I never would have noticed those things without her help."

"It's so exciting. I didn't realize how bad it was until you made it look so good." Laine looked over at the animated group by the coffee maker. "The best thing is knowing that you have friends who care."

"Oh, come on," Colin said. "You always must have had friends."

Laine sighed. "Of course we did when we were young, but my situation is rather like my apartment's. I didn't notice how dusty and shabby my social life was getting. Tonight reminds me how much I've missed pleasant get-togethers just as your drawings make me see how much better my home can be. Time just slipped away from me. I didn't even realize it was happening."

"Well, Madelaine." He gave her name the French pronunciation. "Things are going to change."

"If we don't get home and get some sleep," Midge interrupted, "we're all going to be too tired to change anything. Tomorrow is a workday for all of us."

"True," Bernie groaned. "All those dear little student faces looking up at you."

"Just waiting for you to spout words of wisdom," Andy agreed.

"Ready to sneer if you fail," Colin added.

"You're paranoid," stated a laughing Midge. "We students are only trying to figure out what you're going to put in your exams so we an pass."

"Cynic!" chorused Colin, Andy and Bernie.

"Realist, you mean." Midge pulled on her coat and gathered up her books from the table by the door. "If you don't see me alive tomorrow, everyone remember that I let Bernie drive me home."

Sam ushered his nieces out the door Bernie opened. George followed them with a parting shot to Bernie.

"You be careful with the girl, or I'll be forced to break both your legs."

Bernie carefully lifted Midge's books from her arms. "You go first and I'll follow behind."

Midge rescued her notebook as it slid out of his arms. "You go first so that I can pick up after you. Good night, all!"

Payne gave Laine a quick hug on her way out. "I'm going to put off hunting for that job for the time being. I've always wanted to try my hand at interior decorating. This is my big chance!"

"Let me walk you to your car, Payne," offered Andy. "I'll see about those tiles after classes tomorrow. My brother-in-law owes me for some legal advice. It'll give me a chance to collect on a little debt."

Colin gathered up his designs and put them into a leather folio. He paused at the door and looked at Laine searchingly. "I don't suppose you'd invite me up?"

"No, Colin," Laine said firmly.

"I could check the cat."

"He was thoroughly checked today at the vet's."

He glanced toward the alley where the sound of laughter and chatter could be heard receding into the wet night. "It was fun tonight, wasn't it?"

Laine caught that odd sense of desolation that she'd felt once before. She realized he was the kind of man who would help anyone who came to him. Look at how he'd befriended that bewildered Bernie. She remembered how Payne had been comforted by him as a child. Had anyone ever comforted him? Impulsively she laid her hand on his sleeve.

"It was fun because you gave us all a project that we could share."

The darkness in his eyes dissolved. A warm hand covered hers. "It's typical of you to see it that way, Laine. You're either a total innocent or a very wise woman. Perhaps you're both. Good night, Tower of Strength."

"Good night, Victory," Madelaine whispered.

Moving away from her grasp, he left without looking back. Her eyes followed him as he walked through the dark alley into the light from the street. She felt a sudden urge to call him back. He looked so alone in that dark passage. She shook her head to clear it. Why did she see him that way? Certainly no one else did. He turned the corner and she closed and locked the door.

Leaving on the night lights, Laine opened the door to the upstairs to discover a small gray ball of fuzz waiting for her. "Shadow, poor baby. You wanted to join the party." She picked him up and let him ride on her shoulder. She had to remember to close that upstairs door tightly or one day Shadow would appear in the kitchen. He'd undoubtedly pick the day the health department came to do their inspection.

The apartment wasn't nearly as depressing now that she knew what its future would be. She fed Shadow and took a long bath with him playing along the walnut edge of the tub. They were just about to retire when the phone rang.

It was Payne asking if she could go through the old cupboard in the study. "I saw tons of wonderful things I didn't have time to really get into. I'm sure we can use a lot of those old linens."

Yawning, Laine gave permission for Payne to come in the morning and trudged off to bed. Shadow followed her dutifully. She was just pulling the spread up to her chin when the phone rang again. She and Shadow made another trip to the living room. This time it was Bernie asking if she'd mind if he dropped in around lunchtime to measure for the intercom. She assured him she wouldn't mind. She didn't even make it down the hall before the phone shrilled a third time. Shadow gave up and continued down the hall to bed. Laine tried to keep the irritation out of her voice when she answered.

"I seem to have gotten you out of bed," Colin's velvet voice flowed over her. "I wanted to ask permission to..."

"You have carte blanche to visit any time between the hours of six in the morning and ten in the evening to measure, plan or demolish whatever you wish in the apartment," Laine said, forestalling his request. "Please tell that to everyone else. I love you all, but if I don't get some sleep I'll still be in bed when you come."

"What's wrong with that?" he asked suggestively.

"It would frighten all of you. Without a proper amount of sleep, I resemble the Loch Ness Monster. Thank you, Colin, and good night." Laine gently replaced the receiver and buried the phone under two cushions and assorted pillows. She barely had the strength to push Shadow over before she fell into bed.

The next day sped by. When George arrived early to make the beef stew for lunch, Laine was just pulling the morning croissants out of the oven.

"Sam and I made up our new schedule for the next two weeks." He blithely took a spoon out of the drawer and stirred the beef stock. "You can keep an eye on us, but we want you to enjoy yourself. I'll get the chops ready for dinner. Sam will be in to do the mushroom sauce at four. I'll leave at six after we start serving. Okay?"

Andy ran in to measure something about that time, so Laine gave in graciously. Midge and Bernie rushed in and out between classes. Payne arrived to sort through the old cupboard. Around midmorning Laine brought a pot of tea upstairs to discover Payne and Shadow happily burrowing about in piles of dusty materials.

Payne's gray eyes lighted up at the offer of tea. She carefully extricated herself from a pile of materials. "Laine, do you have any idea of the treasures you had hidden away in this cupboard? Look at this. This is one of the original Rose Lattice patterns. It came out in the early 1900s. My mother paid a fortune for this for her morning room. You have almost ten yards of it here."

Laine peered at the old chintz with pink and red roses climbing up a green crisscross pattern. "I remember that. My grandmother used it to cover some old cushions."

"Old cushions!" groaned Payne. She carefully threaded her way through the stacks of material. Shadow stood up and stretched. Payne scooped him up on the way to the door. "You must go through this with me, Laine. There are hundreds of dollars worth of antique linens. I found a crocheted bedspread that would be perfect for your mother's room." She exchanged Shadow for a cup of tea. "I know several women who'd pay a premium price for any of the linens you don't want. Especially people restoring those old Victorian houses on the lake. The work on these linens is exquisite!"

They were interrupted by a yell from Andy. "Help!"

They found him struggling up the stairs clutching a box of tiles. "I got extra in case we broke some. Colin said to get the old-fashioned black and white. Where do you want them?"

He hauled up several more boxes while the women decided that they should be stored in what would be Emilie's room. Andy fell into the old armchair, causing the broken spring to extend five more inches.

"I'm bushed. Can I scrounge a quick meal from the kitchen? This is my lunch hour. I knew I should've taken up jogging."

Laine led them down to the kitchen and left them deep in discussion about the perils of too little exercise versus too much while they devoured stew and rolls. Lunch sped by with its usual complement of students, instructors and shoppers. Laine helped change the dining room for dinner while she mulled over an idea. In the kitchen she found that Andy had been replaced by Bernie, who was wolfing down a large bowl of stew, and Payne was still there. He looked up cheerfully.

"I thought I'd do the drilling during the hours when you're closed. Your customers won't be bothered that way."

"That was thoughtful of you, Bernie." Laine ladled herself some stew.

"Well, actually, Colin told me that if I did anything to upset your work schedule, he'd throw me off the work force."

Laine sat down facing the worried brown eyes. "I really appreciate this. The intercom will save me a lot of running up and down stairs."

He brightened. "It'll be installed by tonight. You wait and see." He gobbled the rest of his food and set off to work.

"Don't forget to keep track of the bills," Laine reminded him.

"Oh, this is just a bit of this and that from some watchamacallits. I haven't bought anything. The nice parts that show I got from a friend in return for a favor. Didn't cost me anything, so why should you pay for nothing."

Payne's mouth opened, shut and opened again as she leaned over to Laine. "Did you understand anything he just said?"

Laine swallowed hard to keep from choking. "The terrible thing is that I understood him perfectly. He just said that what he's doing is for free and don't embarrass him by discussing money."

"He did?" Payne looked confused.

"Stick around, Payne, and you'll learn to speak Bernie-ese along with the rest of us."

Laine took this time to discuss with Payne the idea she had formulated during her lunch duty. Since Marshield's Import Store also sold antiques and oddities, Laine wondered if they could offer some of what Payne referred to as their treasures to the young couple to sell.

"After all, selling is their profession and I'd love to help them if I could. They could sell the stuff on consignment if they want to. Also, anything we could buy from them would be appreciated." Laine explained about how tough the Marshields had been having it.

The afternoon passed with Laine, Payne and Joy Marshield companionably going over linens and furniture, the sound of Bernie's drilling and hammering in the background. The aromatic smell of the mushroom sauce for the chops drifted up from the kitchen. Even the sound of Shadow's piteous meowing from the bathroom where he'd been locked away didn't dampen Joy's enthusiasm. Payne had promised to call anyone she knew who might be interested in the materials and linens, and she knew quite a few people. Joy dreamily ran her hand over the old spindle-backed chairs that Laine had always hated and smiled.

"I know just the customer for these. She has an entire room done in this period."

"What is that period?" Payne asked.

"I don't know." Joy laughed. "Frank calls it 'early American ghastly,' but this woman is crazy about it. I'll get you a hundred dollars per chair minus our twenty-percent commission, Laine."

Laine gasped. "Is that honest?"

"Someone else would charge her more for them. These chairs are in great shape."

"That's because they're so miserably uncomfortable," Laine said. "Those spindles kill your back."

When Midge arrived to prepare for the evening, Joy and Payne left to tell Frank about their windfall. They promised to return later to transport the treasures to the shop next door.

"I won't be lifting since I'm four months along, but maybe Bernie or someone could help Frank," Joy suggested. She laughed at their confounded expressions. "I know I don't show much yet. He, or she, is due in June, so I really appreciate your thinking of us, Laine. Every little bit really counts now with the baby on the way."

Midge nodded understandingly. "I have some of Joey's baby clothes if you'd like to borrow them, Joy. Babies grow so fast. It seems a shame that they don't get more use out of their clothes."

Joy's eyes lighted up. "Midge, that would be fantastic. I was an only child, so I don't have any siblings to borrow from. And we don't have any relatives out here." She colored and looked at her hands. "I don't mean to imply that we're charity cases."

Midge put her arm around the petite woman. "Hey, you don't need to be embarrassed. I didn't have a cent to buy Joey's baby things. They were all provided by Laine. There are a lot of French meals in those little garments."

"That's right," chimed in Laine. "You take those clothes, Joy Marshield. I like to get my money's worth."

"You two are terrific," Joy said with a catch in her voice.

"That's what they call us," Midge pronounced. "The terrific twins."

"It's better than the terrible twins," Laine agreed. We'd better hurry or dinner is going to be short two hostesses."

"I'll bring the stuff over this weekend, Joy. It's up in the attic. Okay?" Midge yelled over her shoulder as Laine pushed her toward the bedroom to change.

The rest of the evening flew by. In between customers Laine and Midge planned a baby shower for Joy. Laine was delighted to see Midge take such an interest in Joy and her baby. Like Laine, Midge had made few friends outside of the family. Joy and Midge would be good for each other. Laine was pleased with everything and everyone.

She was unaware of a pair of cinnamon eyes watching her intently through the window in the swinging door between the kitchen and dining room. Laine didn't realize that her inner glow made her look especially beautiful this night.

Chapter Six

At ten o'clock that night after all the customers had gone, a crashing and scraping began above the kitchen. Laine looked toward the ceiling and then at Payne and Joy who were sitting at the kitchen table.

"Colin said the bathroom had to be done first because it's the most necessary," reported Payne. "Come and look at Joy's catalog, Laine. She's found the perfect dining-room table."

"It's only a reproduction, but the price is reasonable and we can get it for you wholesale," Joy added.

"It sounds like an army up there," Midge said, grimacing. "It's a good thing that the laundry next door uses their upper floor only for storage."

"Frank couldn't resist getting in on the project," Joy confided. "He loves fixing things." She looked shyly at the other women. "He hasn't had much time to make friends because of the shop. He's really enjoying himself."

Sam finished his cleaning and paused at the door on his way out. "I left a couple of pies for the work force, Miss Laine. See you tomorrow!"

A particularly loud crash made Laine jump and she wondered if the ceiling was going to withstand the onslaught. Payne and Joy assured her that all breakables had been moved to a safe spot and that her bedroom was untouched. It would be the last room done so her lifestyle would be altered as little as possible.

Payne and Joy worked on ideas and pored over catalogs while Laine worked on menus for the coming week and Midge did her homework. They knew the men would call them if help was needed. Until then the best thing was to stay out of the way. Shadow's meows could be heard coming from Laine's bedroom where he had been safely placed out of harm's way.

The male safari that appeared an hour later with boxes of old maroon tiles for the dumpster in the alley was greeted by the delicious smells of warmed-up pie and coffee. They made a production out of brushing the dust off each other, and Bernie threatened them with death if they messed up the kitchen sink in which he'd taken a proprietory interest having once cleaned it.

It was a cheerful, laughing group that tromped off to their various homes after much joking around the old table. As usual, Bernie took Midge home, and the rest of the weary helpers departed, leaving Colin alone with Laine.

"They seemed to enjoy themselves so much." Laine was amazed at the high spirits of these people who worked all day and into the night.

"They did," Colin affirmed.

"I owe everyone so much."

"Stop that! Bernie is delighted because he gets to be around the beautiful Mignon and do work he loves doing. Payne is happy to be away from a dreary home and to be of use. Frank was dying of loneliness with little or no chance to make friends because of his shop. Joy loves being fawned over by you and Midge because of the baby. Andy feels he's paying you back for some of his free meals. Everyone's happy. Why worry about it?"

"I worry about all of you. How can you work all day and night?"

"I don't use my hands during the day, Laine. I use my brains. In fact this kind of work is relaxing. It gets rid of a lot of tension."

"Doesn't it interfere with your writing?"

"So what? There are more books than we need in the world anyway." He quirked one of his upswept eyebrows at her. "Are you trying to get rid of me, Laine? I thought I was behaving exceptionally well for me."

"I don't want you to suffer under any misconceptions. I'm grateful, but that won't change my life-style or my principles." Laine realized that she sounded like a prude, but she'd rather be hung for a lamb than a sheep.

"Lovely Madelaine." Colin sighed, leaning back. "I wouldn't attempt to corrupt those iron principles of yours, but I'm certainly after that rotten life-style. You're too young to bury youself in that mausoleum upstairs."

Laine noticed a streak of plaster dust across his high cheekbone. She almost reached up to brush it away but caught herself in time.

"I didn't have a lot of choice about my life-style."

He turned his head to look her square in the eye. "Didn't you? Why didn't you look for a partner who could back you so that you could hire another cook and have a normal workday? Why aren't you doing that now?

I can see that you were dealt a certain hand in the game of life, Laine, but no one made you play that hand the way you did. You chose to go it alone, didn't you? Where's it written that that was required of you?"

She felt impaled under his steady gaze. She drew in a breath and replied honestly. "Yes, I guess I did. I've never thought of it that way before."

He unfolded himself from the chair. "Think about it, Laine. Are you worried about us, or are you worried about your pride suffering because we're lending you a helping hand? See you tomorrow," he tossed over his shoulder as he went through the door.

Laine was stunned by his statement. He'd gone and she was alone. The ticking of the old clock seemed deafening in the silence he'd left behind him.

Other than her father and grandmother, no person had ever made Laine question herself as much as this man had. It seemed as though every time they met, he left her examining her life.

Was she too proud to accept a helping hand from friends? Had she become so independent that she felt she could do everything alone?

Laine sat back and considered her position. On the other hand, was Colin trying to throw her off guard by questioning her independence? Why did that man have such a genius for getting to her?

Colin had spearheaded the entire redecorating project. The others accepted his leadership easily. Why did Laine resist Colin so much? She couldn't answer this confusing question. Suddenly she was overcome with fatique. She locked up the kitchen and went upstairs to receive Shadow's hysterical greeting.

"Oh, you poor little thing," she crooned to the quivering kitten. "We're both in a state of confusion about where we're supposed to be." She lifted the gray animal up and looked him in the eye. "Never mind. Your home is wherever I am. I promise."

The rest of the week rushed by in a train of small decisions and minor traumas involving decorating. The new black-and-white bath was elegant. However, Laine found that the only two rooms she could function in were the bath and her room because the rest of the apartment had succumbed to the attack of the Friends of Laine Society. By Friday the divider that created the new dining room had been installed and Bernie was fast creating electronic magic.

Saturday Laine was unable to take any time off. The lunch crowd was unusually large and she was planning broiled tournedos in béarnaise sauce for dinner. It took all three cooks to handle the filets mignons. Laine spent the afternoon creating her blancmange for the dessert. She refused to prepare the pudding in a large mass because it lost its flavor and the cornstarch seemed to lose its thickening power in large batches. Thus she created the custard only thirty servings at a time. After five hours of custard making, three hundred little yellow molds resided in the refrigerator. Later the custards would be unmolded, displaying a dainty fleur-de-lis pattern on top, and returned to the cold nestled on the crystal plates with their chocolate sugar cookies as a color contrast.

Laine was aware of her friends' coming in and out, drinking coffee and eating soup or chili by the door, but she had little time to chat. This expensive meal was only served once a month, so her complete attention was called for.

Delicately Sam and George shaped the filet strips and surrounded them with bacon, ready for broiling. Mei and

Gschu squeezed whipped potatoes through pastry bags into tiny boats and added the Gruyère cheese to each.

Midge appeared dressed for dinner smelling faintly of turpentine overlaid with her favorite perfume to hand Laine the shallots, peppercorns, tarragon and chervil for the delicate Bernaise sauce that made people come from the distant suburbs on this special night.

When the sauce reached its proper consistency, Laine set it over the hot water in the giant double broiler and rushed upstairs to change. She appreciated the path that had been cleared from the door to the bathroom. Laine pulled on her white dress, gave Shadow a pat and a promise, and ran past Colin, Andy, Payne, Frank and Bernie to the stairs. She had her foot on the first step when she realized that the five of them had formed a double line and were saluting her with upraised paintbrushes dipped in white paint.

Laine raised her fingers in a V for the victory sign and ran down the stairs carrying her shoes to the sound of their cheering. What fun these people were. She wished she'd the time to comment on what they'd accomplished that day, but she'd really been too rushed. Slipping on her high heels, she paused to check the sauce once more. George, Sam and the girls were at their stations. Laine stepped into the quiet peace of the dining room and serenely went to greet her first customers.

Most of her patrons were repeats who always tried to make reservations for the night she served her special meal. No one had ever complained about her food when she served tournedos in béarnaise. She'd looked forward to a pleasant evening of satisfied customers. Her heart sank when she saw Payne's mother and father waiting to be seated. Laine had been too busy with the apartment this week to really go over the reservations made by the staff. She greeted the Petersons by name, which seemed to surprise the man but not Beatrice Peterson.

She's come to check up on poor Payne, Laine thought dismally. I wonder if she'll require an inspection of the upstairs as part of the meal. Seating the couple at a table, she left them to the waitress's tender ministrations.

"She'll be hard put to find something wrong with this meal," Laine murmured as she caught Midge's eye and knew her twin had recognized them, also.

Midge whispered in her ear, "This is going to be an expensive charity if she has another attack of vapors."

"Her husband will undoubtedly send a check with Payne to cover it if she does. It's really tragic, Midge. We'll just have to grin and bear it."

"Money doesn't make up for humiliation." Midge looked grim. "I don't think anyone has explained that to Mr. Peterson."

Laine tried to keep her eyes on the Petersons to check Beatrice's response to the food, but her attention was claimed by a large group of women who'd taken the party room for their monthly dinner meeting. There was a slight problem of four extra guests.

"I know it's an imposition, my dear, but when they heard where the meeting was to be held, they insisted on coming. You can squeeze in just four more, can't you?"

Laine and the waitresses added another small table to the long table and set four more places. They were prepared. This had happened many times before with groups. The extra services had already been readied at the serving table in the room. Actually they could accommodate as many as eight extra persons. It was Laine's ability to adjust to the group's demands without unpleasantness that made them come back to Maman's again and again. When the women were seated and chattering over their salads, Laine returned to the main room to find the Petersons well into their meal. She'd almost passed their table when an imperative gesture from Beatrice stopped her. Laine turned to face the older woman, trying not to feel like a condemned criminal.

"I wanted to tell you that this béarnaise is the best I've tasted in years. You may not have good eggplant, but your meat is exceptional, Miss Morgan. I must compliment you. I'm looking forward to your blancmange."

"Thank you, Mrs. Peterson." Laine smiled down at the cool gray eyes. "I'm so glad that we've redeemed ourselves. Please continue to enjoy your meal."

Laine hastened over to Midge. "Did you hear?"

Midge smiled smugly. "I certainly did!"

"Do you think I answered her compliment appropriately?"

Midge grinned openly. "You sounded exactly like a nice twelve-year-old speaking to a maiden aunt who's just given her a blouse two sizes too small. It was perfect."

"Don't be snide, Mignon. I was trying to be friendly without overcompensating. I didn't sound unfriendly, did I? I don't want to get Payne in trouble. I don't want to hurt that poor woman's feelings, either." Laine frowned at Midge.

"Colin's right, Laine. You worry too much. You were absolutely correct in a properly professional way. Stop worrying."

The arrival of another party ended the conversation. What did Midge mean, Colin was right? Since when had Midge discussed her sister with Colin? Laine had the peculiar feeling that her sister and friends were railroading her into something. She knew they would do it for her own benefit. She just hoped she'd feel that it was beneficial.

The customers loved to linger after this kind of meal so Laine and Midge weren't able to close up until later than usual. When they entered the kitchen, they found all of their friends politely waiting for them. Payne was helping Sam broil their steaks while Bernie was hauling salads to the table. Andy was savoring a roll and ignoring Frank's teasing.

Joy greeted the twins. "We've been invited to dinner by your cook."

The wet hair of the men and the shiny look of everyone's faces attested to the fact that they had just cleaned up. Bernie's thick hair stood up in cowlicks as he plopped salads at everyone's place. By common consent, Colin sat at the head of the table. Midge took the chair between Joy and Bernie, leaving Laine to take the foot.

George put more rolls in front of Andy. "We haven't been able to help much with the work upstairs, Miss Laine. We felt that the least we could do was to stay late and feed your crew."

Laine slipped off her heels and took in all of the amiable faces around her. "I love you all and thank you. I'm sorry I didn't have a chance to look at your work today. It was a little hectic."

"It's worth a day of work to eat one of your fabulous meals," Frank asserted gallantly. "Those delicious smells have been tantalizing me all night long. I almost lost control and rushed down to ambush one of your people."

"Eat up," George boomed. "You've earned it! Sam and I went up to look at the place. You've done a terrific job. It's one hundred percent improved."

Even the quiet Sam was enthused about the group's efforts. "It's an elegant place for an elegant lady," he announced.

"I should run up and look." Laine pushed back her chair but was stopped by Colin's words.

"Eat now, look later. You've worked hard all day yourself."

"I never realized how much work there is in cooking," Bernie blurted out over his salad. I don't think I even saw Laine stop running today."

George pulled out the meat and Payne served the steaks from the broiling pan. "She works too hard." Payne set Andy's meat in front of him.

Sam put the sauce on the table. "That's true," he agreed.

"This was an unusual night because of this particular meal." Laine watched Sam serve the boats of potatoes. "You're all putting in a lot of extra hours."

"We're having fun." Joy tasted her food. "Oh, this is marvelous!"

"I don't have to put sauce on my meat, do I?" Bernie grumbled.

"Only a total barbarian would reject this béarnaise," Colin snapped, giving Bernie a glare.

"No, Bernie." Laine rescued him. "You don't have to put the sauce on your filet. Enjoy it as you like it."

The moments of silence complemented Laine's cooking skills. No one wanted to interrupt their meal with conversation. It wasn't until the blancmange was served that everyone allowed their taste buds to come up for air. The men were loud in their praise. Payne looked positively transported. Joy had the expression of a contented kitten. Mignon looked at her sister languidly.

"You know, Laine, sometimes I forget what a genius you are until I'm reminded. We put so many people through each night. It's been too long since we've had a party for friends. I'd forgotten just how superb you really are."

It's been seven years, Midge, Laine thought to herself but did not voice her thought aloud. It was enough that Midge looked so happy even as she informed Bernie that she could eat her own pudding without his help. Laine went to get Bernie an extra portion to keep him from consuming Mignon's.

After supper the work crew went up to observe Laine's first viewing of their work. Payne admonished Laine "not to expect too much because the curtains and accessories aren't in place yet."

Laine turned on the light and the old chandelier glowed with new fluted chimneys and subtler lamps. The white walls of the living room looked clean and welcoming. The old chair was gone, leaving a space for a new one, but the white shuttered expanse of new wall shone. Bernie hastened to open the shutters and explain the mysteries of the remote-control TV and the stereo. Her few records had been carefully stored in the proper compartments.

Payne pointed to the old daybed with its carved wood sides and back. "Wait until we get the fabrics and the curtains. It'll look a lot brighter."

They led her to the kitchen, which was almost completely redecorated. The walls were white with distressed blue antiquing that exactly matched the blue flowers on the ironstone bowl full of white roses sitting on the homespun blue tablecloth.

"Joy made the curtains," Frank offered proudly.

Laine touched the crisp blue gingham at the windows. Her mother's delft blue-and-white plates had been dusted and hung on a rail that ran around three walls of the room. A blue-and-white braided rug lay under the small trestle table with its straight-back chairs.

"Oh!" breathed Laine, admiring the white shutters at the windows that would shut out the dreary days. Even the fixture over the table had the blue and white colors in stained glass. Bernie was giving a running commentary.

"Midge found the bowl. Colin got the flowers. Joy made the curtains. I traded an old computer for the fixture. Payne found the rug and the tablecloth. Frank put up the rail for the plates. Andy put the blue and white tiles around the sink and Colin painted."

"Oh!" Laine gasped as she looked at the wonderful kitchen in amazement. Everyone laughed.

Mignon translated for her. "She likes it."

"I love it!"

Even at two in the morning the rest of the rooms were wonderfully full of light because of the new paint. The dining room was empty, but the bedrooms had their beds and chests. Laine noticed that the wedding chest had been moved to her new room. The study still had the old cupboard and her father's desk. She told the group over and over how much she loved it and nearly fainted when Joy handed her a check for seven hundred dollars.

"That's for the stuff we sold so far," Joy said, smiling. "There's more to come."

"People paid so much for old sheets and materials?" Laine was astounded.

"Your great-grandmother did wonderful lacework on those old sheets, and she used the old thick cotton that can't be bought any more. Besides, they like to show off their antique bedding to their friends. It's a matter of prestige." Joy assured Laine that they'd taken out their commission.

"It just doesn't seem honest," Laine murmured.

"There she goes again!" Midge nudged her sister. "You're a pillar of iron when the going is rough, but give you a little prosperity and you fall to pieces."

"You can give me that money, and Joy and I will hunt for the curtains and drapes for the living room and order the dining-room set and..." Payne was interrupted by Colin.

"I think we've impressed her with our genius enough for one night. Let her catch her breath. She might like to spend that money on some personal renovation. Perhaps a dress that isn't black or white?"

"Come on, Payne." Andy led the tall girl to the door. "I'll take you home. Only you've got to promise not to discuss drapes. I'll fall asleep over the wheel." He pulled Payne through the doorway as she was still making plans to meet with Joy at the shop on Monday to order the dining-room curtains.

"I won't see you at the early service tomorrow, Laine," Joy yawned. "We'll sleep in until the noon service. I have to sleep for two, you know." She gave Laine a quick hug and exited with Frank.

Midge organized her clothes and handed her case to Bernie. He managed to take it without incident. She looked at Colin and Laine. "See, he's improving. He didn't jerk my wrist out of joint."

"Bernie, thank you for the entertainment center and the intercom. I'll think of you every time I use it." Laine patted Bernie's shoulder. He looked at Midge.

"How come you don't say nice things to me like Laine does?"

"I asked you to lunch tomorrow and I'm cooking," Midge retorted. "If you knew how much I hate to cook, you'd know how much I appreciate you. Go!"

Colin was left looking musingly at Laine. "You know, it would be pleasant to see you in the morning or to have coffee with you in the afternoon. It seems as though we're always facing each other at two in the morning. You're usually tired and worried about your virtue. I'm a little wilted around the edges myself."

"After all you did today, that's not surprising. Why don't you come over to Midge's tomorrow for lunch? I promise to be wide awake and in good conversational form."

He started toward her and Laine found that she had no desire to move away. Suddenly the intercom above their heads gave a squawk and the voice of Officer Dodd grated into the room.

"Laine, are you up there? Did you know that your door was unlocked?"

Laine stepped away from Colin and flipped the switch on her kitchen wall as Bernie had taught her. "Hi, Charlie. We're just finishing up. I have one more person to let out."

"I'll wait then," said Charlie's voice. "I want to make sure you're locked up properly on a Saturday night."

Colin smiled ruefully but didn't continue with his previous plans. He simply touched the back of her neck as she started down the stairs ahead of him. She stopped on the step, aware of the long fingers on her nape. His lips briefly caressed her ear.

"One day I'll have more than a few minutes alone with you, Madelaine. You won't be surrounded by crowds of people, and you won't have a policeman waiting in the wings. You'll have to face me by yourself. It'll be interesting to see how you handle a man, one on one."

Charlie's cheerful, dried-apple face greeted them in the kitchen. "Oh, I didn't know you had a gentlemen upstairs with you or I wouldn't have worried about you. I thought it was one of your lady friends or Midge. Come to think of it, George did mention that you had a boyfriend now."

Laine caught Colin's amused expression with mortification. If her friends didn't stop throwing this man at her, she'd die of embarrassment.

"She was perfectly safe, believe me," Colin informed Charlie.

"Charlie," Laine said, performing a red-faced introduction.

"Oh yeah." Charlie wrung Colin's hand. "Midge says you're the fella who does all those snazzy history books. My wife is crazy about them. Wait till I tell her that Laine has snagged herself a real writer. She'll be tickled pink. Of course, nobody's good enough for Laine here, but she'll approve of you."

Oh stop, Charlie, Laine prayed silently.

"Laine has to be explained 'cause she never was one to ring her own bell." Charlie ignored Laine's silent plea. "Why, when the twins were teens there were flocks of guys around here. I think they're even more beautiful today, don't you?"

"I do." Colin kept his face perfectly straight.

"Midge was the more outgoing, but she's suffered a lot of tragedy. Do you have a friend for her, young fella? I'd sure like to see the twins settled before I retire."

"As a matter of fact, I do have a friend." Colin gave Laine a wicked look over Charlie's head. "His name is Bernie." He started out the door with Charlie on his heels. "He's teaching at the university, too. Midge seems very interested."

Laine slammed the lock into place as the door closed behind them. She'd visions of Charlie telling Colin the story of her life, including the time she and Midge had gotten lost on the university campus at the age of four and had gotten sick from eating the ice-cream cones Charlie had bought for them on the way home.

Someone had filled Shadow's dish with filet and by the time Laine was ready for bed, the little cat was so full he could barely climb on the bed. She looked at the smug little pansy face and smoothed his whiskers back.

"It's been a day and a half, Shadow. I'll bet you're glad it's over. Now you've got the run of the apartment again. I'll miss the excitement though, even if you don't." After a short purr Shawdow fell into a doze with all four paws in the air and his head resting on Laine's pillow.

She fell asleep with Shadow's fur tickling her ear, reminding her of the whisper of the man on the dark stairs and his warning.

Chapter Seven

Laine was packing her usual Sunday lunch hamper for the family when someone knocked at the kitchen door. She opened it to find Colin, handsome in a brown corduroy suit, still managing to look crisp in spite of the eternal drizzle.

"I'm picking you and the Marshields up for lunch. Mignon's orders! Did you really throw up all over Charlie's new uniform?"

"I was four years old and he'd fed us too many ice-cream cones," Laine stated defensively. "Half of the mess was Midge's. He should have known better."

He followed her to the table. "Bernie's already helping at Midge's. Actually he took Joey some more games."

Laine smiled. "Keeping Joey out from under Midge's feet is helping."

"I like that fuzzy sweater you're wearing. It's the same colors as your eyes."

"It's called brown heather." Laine handed him a plate of rolls and a jar of her mother's homemade jam. "It's not black or white, you'll notice."

"You look lovely in your uniforms." Colin spread jam on a roll. "I just happen to prefer you in color."

Laine put the cover on the hamper. "Is Midge having a party?"

"It's a thank-you to your crew from her. She wanted to contribute something special. I take it the Marshields did go to the late service?"

"They'll be home in about ten minutes." Laine jumped as a pathetic meow issued from the intercom. "I forgot to turn it off and Shadow can hear us talking." She switched off the intercom and turned to find Colin staring at her.

"What's wrong?" She was struck by his serious expression.

"You left your hair down."

She touched her shoulder-length hair. "Yes."

"You look like one of my college students with that pleated skirt and your hair swinging loose like that."

"Well, Mr. Laird. I'm not a student. Are Payne and Andy coming?"

"Does Andy ever pass up a free meal?"

"He's lonely. He doesn't come just for the meals. Be fair."

"I don't feel like being fair about Andy." Colin spread a third roll. "We're all lonely. I'll bet it doesn't bother you to be alone with Andy."

"No, it doesn't because I know he'll behave himself and..." Laine hesitated.

"And?"

"He's trustworthy." Laine wasn't going to admit to Colin that Andy had never been a serious temptation. "Payne is a very attractive girl," she ventured.

"She's a nice kid. No one in that family paid her any attention, but I always thought she had a lot more going for her than Jim. Beatrice and John put all of their ambitions into their son and forgot Payne. That's probably why she turned out so well."

"She says nice things about you, too." Laine sat across from him. "She said you were her first love."

"Payne was a gangly little kid with big gray eyes. She was always getting hurt by Jim or the other kids. Someone had to look out for her. Don't get any ideas, Laine. You aren't going to get rid of me that easily. Payne was like a little sister to me. That's all."

"You have a great deal in common, don't you? You both come from old moneyed families. You had a different life from most of us. I'd think that would count for something."

Colin sternly looked her in the eye. "Jim had the same upbringing and ended up badly. Payne had all of the advantages and is frightened of her own shadow. I had all of the advantages and grew up totally isolated with various housekeepers for company. What would you like to count that for, Laine?"

"Were you really disinherited?"

"Payne has been talking, I see. No, my father had started the proceedings, but they weren't completed when the accident happened. I think he only meant to scare me, but I had a scholarship so I didn't scare easily."

"What was your mother like?"

Colin snapped the lid on the jam jar impatiently. "I really don't know. I barely knew her. She was a pretty woman with a light, high voice that broke easily. She always wore floating things because my father preferred them. She flitted in and out of my life like a moth or a holiday. She never seemed to care if I was there or not. She was merely my father's appendage. Your mother is more real to me, and I've only met her once. My father was someone who gave or withheld the money for what I wanted. He had certain expectations for me and that was all he wanted. At twenty-three it gave me a great deal of satisfaction to thwart those expectations. He was dead by the time I was twenty-five."

"Oh, Colin." The coldness with which Colin had related his story made it all the more terrible.

"Don't waste time on pity, Madelaine." Colin's face was closed and hard. "That kind of upbringing isn't as damaging as you might suppose. Jim was adored and cosseted all of his life. What good did it do him? I learned very young to be independent emotionally and intellectually. I knew how to stand and fight for myself. I had to investigate my own resources much earlier than most children, but it gave me a head start as an adult. I missed the loving family of your background, but then I wasn't trapped into years of self-sacrifice as you've been. Who's to say which of us is better off? I'm financially solvent and always have been. Can you say the same? What was the advantage of throwing your life away to save the family? Midge is going her own way and leaving you in the lurch. Your mother, as Charlie informed me last night, never comes near this place. What have you saved?"

"The people I love," Laine answered simply.

"Why didn't they love you well enough to save you?"

The invisible wall that Laine had sensed between herself and Colin suddenly seemed to have grown too high to reach over. How could she explain the situation to him in a way he would understand? She couldn't. She could only tell the truth.

"My grandmother used to explain these things well. She'd say that sometimes our heart's desire isn't what would be best for us at all. I could have walked away from the family and gone on to be a Cordon Bleu. I might have been able to ignore my mother in the hospital or my sister in a sanitarium. Perhaps I would have forgotten about Joey being raised in a foster home. Suppose I became a brilliant chef and made lots of money. Then what would I have had? Would success have loved me as my mother had throughout my childhood? Could things have replaced my sister's caring and the years of sharing? Could the praises of customers have made up for missing the dearness that is Joey? How could I have turned my back on my family? How much money would it take to replace the people who love us and whom we love? A thousand dollars? A million?"

"You could marry and have your own family," Colin suggested.

"I hope to, but not at the expense of another family." Laine reached out and laid her hand over his. "You must understand that everyone doesn't have the same strength at the same time. I had what was needed these past few years. There may come a time when I'll need their strength. That's the nature of loving. It's not fifty-fifty, Colin. Sometimes it's sixty-forty or twenty-eighty. It depends on how great the need is. Their need was greater."

His hand turned and eveloped hers in his grasp. "How do you know when your need will be greater? Won't you always see someone else's need first? Can I get in a bid for need at this time, Laine?"

"What do you need, Colin?"

"You."

"I'm your friend." Laine let her hand rest easily in his.

"You're everyone's friend."

"It's a good start. Colin, please be a friend for now. I have so many things to sort out. You make it hard for me to think."

"That's the best news I've heard all week. I do have some affect on you."

Laine smiled into the rust-colored eyes. "You were right about Andy. I'm not afraid to be alone with him because I know his intentions are strictly honorable."

His eyes showed gold glints in appreciation. "That's even better news."

A rapping on the door announced the Marshields' arrival, but Colin was slow to release her. He raised her hand, turned it palm up and kissed it. "Friends. For now."

She dared not look back as she went to let Joy and Frank in.

The day passed pleasantly. Midge and Emilie had baked a turkey with all the trimmings. After dinner the men sank into oblivion in the living room while the women attacked the kitchen. Midge gave Joy the boxes of baby clothes as she'd promised. Joy crooned over each tiny garment. Laine left Emilie and Midge chatting with Joy about babies and went out for a walk with Joey. They discussed serious things like Shadow's health, the problems of first-grade math and the wonders of soccer. Colin found them on the front porch deep in a discussion about acquiring a pet that grandmama wasn't allergic to. He promptly suggested fish, snakes or a turtle. Grandmama loathed snakes and fish demanded a lot of attention, but turtles, especially the large box turtles, were quite easy to take care of and didn't smell.

Colin promised that he'd talk to a friend in the zoology department and would get back to Joey if his mother and grandmother gave permission. Joey immediately left to secure that permission while Colin and Laine talked about the need for pets for a child. Colin had had a turtle as a child because it was all he was allowed because his father detested dogs and cats. The main advantage of the turtle was that it didn't have fur for Emilie to be concerned about.

Joey was back in a flash, begging Colin to tell his mother and grandmother about the wonders of turtledom. "I've almost convinced them but I need your help." Colin followed Joey in to do battle for the rights of a boy and a turtle and Payne took his place.

"It's been a wonderful day, Laine. Thank you so much for including me."

"Midge did all the planning for today, Payne. I'm still thinking about a way to reward you all for the work."

"Wait until it's really finished," Payne protested. "Then we can celebrate the end product."

"I like it so much, I may be adding to it for years." Laine laughed. "We'd never have our party."

"Laine." Payne's expression was the same as when they'd first met. "I'm going to ask you something, and I want you to seriously consider it. My feelings won't be hurt if you refuse. No, I'm lying. I'll probably go into a decline if you refuse but I'll understand."

"Good heavens, Payne. What is it?" Laine wondered if Payne were going to ask her about Colin's intentions or their relationship.

Payne took a deep breath and plunged in. "I want to buy into Maman's as a partner. Midge and I were talking about how you'd have to get a partner, since she isn't going to come into the business. I wondered if it couldn't be me. I know I lack experience, but I'd learn fast." She rushed on to name what to Laine was an astronomical sum. Laine looked so shocked at the amount of money offered that Payne immediately panicked.

"I know it's a surprise. I know I'm being pushy. Of course you want to find someone with more to bring to the business. I'm not as good a cook as you, but I'm sure I could learn from you, Laine. I could come up with more money if that isn't enough. I talked to my lawyer and he felt it was a fair offer for an established business that was growing, but I could come up with more..."

"Payne, stop." Laine's head was whirling. "The offer is more than enough."

"Then it's me. You don't want me." Payne looked stricken.

Laine put her arm around the shivering girl next to her. "I like you very much. You're my friend whether I accept your offer or not, Payne. I just want to make sure you really understand what you might be getting into. That's too much money to put into something that's a favor for a friend or a sudden enthusiasm. We're talking about a lot of work." Laine continued on, telling Payne of the hours, the problems, the mistakes she'd made and what she planned for the restaurant. She reminded Payne of her parents' possible displeasure.

"I'm twenty-five years old, Laine. You were the one who advised me to find work. I've found work. I could help you cut down those long days. I've always wanted to work in a small specialty place like Maman's. You said 'go for it.' Well, I'm going for it. After all, I'm only three years younger than you and Midge."

"Payne, you have the money and the freedom to go and become a real Cordon Bleu. You're in a position where you don't have to make compromises."

Payne looked miserably at her long hands twisting in her lap. "No, Laine, I couldn't. I'm so painfully shy around most people that I'm practically a zombie. I tried a professional school in New York. I had the talent, but I was so horribly tongue-tied...I was so nervous that I couldn't hold a spoon properly. It should be funny but it wasn't. I cried every night for two months and then packed up and slunk back home."

Laine knew she had to give Payne some kind of immediate answer. Payne had suffered enough in her life. Laine wouldn't add to that suffering one iota if she could avoid it. She tried to think clearly and logically. Then she remembered what she'd said to Colin just that morning about love being given when it was needed. She squeezed Payne's shoulders.

"Midge and I always wanted a younger sister. If you really want to be involved in the business, I'd love to have you for a partner, Payne. You're on."

"Do you really mean it?" Payne's eyes misted over.

"How could I resist an offer like that?" Laine laughed at her friend and fished out a dry tissue to tuck into Payne's hand. "I just wanted you to know what you'd be getting into. I wouldn't want to trap you with the false impression that it's all fun and games in the kitchen."

"I was good in math, too." Payne blinked away her tears. "Midge can oversee me with the books until she feels I'm competent, but what are you going to do about the checkout counter? I couldn't face all those people every night."

Laine thought for a moment. "I think Betty might be ready for that spot by summer. She knows all of our evening customers and they like her. I'll shift Janet to evenings and we'll hire a new waitress for lunches. How do you like that, partner?"

"I like it very much, partner." Payne's face was transformed by happiness. "Can we go tell the others?"

Everyone thought the new partnership was a fine idea. Andy heartily approved and asked if he'd still be welcome in the kitchen. Colin smiled his crooked smile and congratulated them. Bernie, of course, asked Payne if she put "all those sauces on the meat." Payne assured him that he could have his meat without.

The rest of the evening was spent discussing the new partnership and the apartment.

Bernie looked devotedly at Emilie. "Wait until you see it, Mrs. Morgan. It's completely changed."

"I'll come and see it when Laine has it all finished." Emilie patted Bernie's hand. "I couldn't come before because it reminded me too much of Maurice and all our happy years. I'm glad you set aside my mother's old room for me. I'd be much happier staying there than the master bedroom."

Payne and Joy launched into a detailed description of what the bedroom would look like. They told Joey about the daybed in the living room that was just his size.

"You'll have to lock up the feline," Emilie reminded Laine. "I'm sure he's charming but my sneezes are not."

Colin and Frank packed the baby clothes into the back of Colin's station wagon and took off with Payne and Andy following right behind them. Laine looked back at Emilie, Midge, Joey and Bernie waving at them from the porch. Bernie looked so protective of the family that she felt a slight twinge. It was time for her to let go of that responsibility. Next year Midge would have a good income of her own. If Bernie continued to take an interest, and he looked good for the whole course, most of Laine's worries would be over. It was obvious that Bernie was fond of Emilie. With the partnership, Laine had to face the fact that she needed to carve a new life for herself.

She leaned her head against the window, watching the drizzle trickle down the glass. It was like graduating from school and looking for a job. The family and the business had been her main concerns for so many years, it was difficult to adjust to new goals. The murmuring of Joy and Frank's light voices punctuated by Colin's baritone as they conversed about the university offerings in evening classes seemed far away.

"Wouldn't that be fun, Laine?" Joy broke into her reverie.

"I'm sorry, I was daydreaming." Laine tried to recall what Joy had said.

"Next year after Payne has taken over some of your hours and the baby is here, we might take some evening classes at the university. I've always wanted to take an art course of some sort. Would you like that? Or maybe we could take one of Colin's history courses?"

"You haven't even had the baby, and you're already making plans to abandon us," Frank teased his wife.

"Nonsense, a woman needs to get away from the house occasionally to keep her other skills up. You wouldn't want me to be one of those women who can't talk about anything except cooking and babies, would you?"

Frank kissed the curls on Joy's forehead. "Whatever makes you happy."

"I don't think I'd want to take a cooking class," Laine said, making them all laugh, "but it might be fun to take an art class."

"You'll notice she didn't even consider the history course," Colin commented.

"I'll read all of your books instead." Laine promised.

Frank laughed. "Wouldn't that make your education a little one-sided?"

"Not if it's the right side," Colin returned. "Learn from the best."

They were all laughing as they pulled into the alley by the Marshields' back door.

"Do come up and see what we've done," Joy begged. "I want to show Laine the baby's room."

The Marshields' apartment was similar to Laine's but smaller. They had only two bedrooms so their office was downstairs. It was a charming home, reflecting the eclectic tastes of its owners and their knowledge of antiques. The colors were cheerful yellows, greens and browns to complement their oak woodwork.

The baby's room had all natural oak furniture, including a big old rocking chair with wide arms and a high back. Laine admired the crib with its spindled rails and carved back.

"It's beautiful, Joy."

"I painted the room yellow so the baby would have a bright day no matter how much rain was outside." Joy patted the yellow-and-white quilt covering the bed. "I really like Seattle, but it was hard to get used to the constant dampness."

"It's the price we pay for the grandeur of Mount Rainier, the lakes and the ocean." Laine rocked in the comfortable rocker. "This is wonderful. I'd love to get a chair like this for my mother's room."

"We'll keep an eye out for one in walnut," Joy promised as they went to join the men who were listening to a record from Frank's jazz collection.

Later Frank and Joy walked them down to the alley door and joked about literally seeing her to her own door. "It's lovely to have real neighbors at last," Joy burbled.

"Maybe we can get to know the couple who owns the bookstore on the other side. In the spring we could have a block party."

"Not a bad idea," Laine agreed. "The LeMons were friends of my parents. They get up at five and go to bed at nine. That's why you don't see much of them unless you're buying books. Jules LeMons and my father used to play chess together. It'd be fun to close off the alley some Sunday in the late spring or early summer and have a party. Let's do it!"

She unlocked the door and turned to face Colin. "Thank you for the company and the transportation, Colin. We both have a busy day ahead of us tomorrow. I'm going up to dive into my gorgeous white room with my cat for company and sleep like a log."

"Before you slam the door in my face, I have one request. Next week your mother is spending Sunday at a friend's house. Bernie has asked Midge out for dinner and a movie. She's captured a baby-sitter, so you'll be free. I thought we could have lunch and go to the annual antique show at the armory. We might find some things for the apartment. Frank and Joy said they'd love to join us, if you can break away from your kitchen."

"I'd love to go." Laine smiled at his mock humility.

"I thought you would if you had chaperons," Colin said dryly. "Still, I am narrowing the field down from large to small groups. That's some progress. Good night, Laine." His lips brushed hers in a brotherly kiss. She turned to go but was spun back into his arms and the next kiss was anything but brotherly. He let her go and gently pushed her in the door.

"Sorry about that for your sake, not mine."

The next few weeks rushed by as Payne was initiated into the restaurant business. The apartment was taking shape with accessories and drapes. Colin began to become an integral part of Laine's life.

Payne had been modest in her assessment of her culinary talents. Laine found her to be an extremely inventive cook. She bloomed in Maman's large kitchen and her diffident, shy ways endeared her to the rest of the staff. It was Payne who thought up the idea of the small kabobs that could be dipped in different sauces for the lunch crowd. They proved to be so popular, they became a permanent addition to the lunch menu. Students would buy them wrapped in paper like hot dogs and go off down the street munching them. The catering activities began to expand with Payne's hands there to do some of the extra work.

Laine noticed that she saw a good deal more of Andy since Payne had started working, but she had to admit he showed the girl more masculine protective qualities than he ever had Laine. That was all to the good. Payne needed that kind of reinforcement from a male. In return she was bringing out some of Andy's hidden abilities. Her shyness and modesty made him more sensitive to others and a far more interesting person.

Thanks to Joy, Frank and Colin, the apartment began to take on a look that Midge called "elegant homeness." When Laine laughed at the combination of those two words, Midge sniffed, "That's what it looks like. The quilts and all that blue-and-white homespun make it homey, but the wood and the way it goes together is elegant. What would you call it?"

Laine said she called it home.

Colin found the old-fashioned dressing table that matched the walnut four-poster in her room. "That highboy is fine for storing clothes, but a woman needs a dressing table," he stated authoritively. It was the grandmother of all dressing tables with an immense mirror and tiny drawers up both sides to hold makeup and hair supplies. The middle drawer opened up to reveal felt compartments for special pieces of jewelry. She didn't have the heart to tell him she owned so few pieces that it seemed a waste of space. It came with a small chair that just fit her diminutive height.

"I feel like an empress sitting in front of it," she said, laughing.

"It's about time," he retorted, adjusting the mirror to the right angle.

With Payne and the partnership money in the bank, Laine began alternating weekdays with her partner. She splurged on new clothes for herself and insisted that Midge do the same. She didn't buy one black or white item, but indulged herself in forest greens, chocolate browns and a brilliant topaz. She even bought a red silk dress with puffed sleeves and a swirling skirt for Valentine's Day.

The best surprise was when her dining-room set arrived. The gleam of the walnut table and its ten high-back chairs completed the major furniture for the apartment. She left eight chairs around it permanently and set the other two at either end of the matching sideboard. She was ready to do some personal entertaining and knew who her nine guests were going to be. Valentine's Day fell on a Sunday and it was the perfect day for what Laine had in mind.

Midge was busy with midterms, so Laine elicited Payne's help for the planning. Payne was delighted to be included. "You may not be when you realize what Valentine's Day is to Maman's," Laine cautioned. She related the tradition to Payne. Since Renée Dupré, Emilie's mother, had first started her restaurant for the loggers of

Seattle, Valentine's Day had been the night when romance was celebrated at Maman's.

"That's why the reservations have been in for weeks." Payne had noticed on the reservation board that Saturday night before Valentine's Day had been full for ages.

"Even in our difficult years, that night has always been full." Laine outlined the events of that special evening. She showed Payne the condiment dishes in the shape of crystal hearts. "The candlesticks were created by an artist friend of my father's. He's the same man who etched the stemware for the governor's mansion." She displayed the tall candlesticks with the engraved hearts and ribbons twining around the base. "We only use them on Valentine's Day."

Payne assured Laine that she'd be up to double duty if Laine was. The Valentine's Day dinner at Maman's was one of the most expensive meals of the year. This was due in large part to the waste inherent in the menu. Mr. Jones had ordered the special chocolate bonbons wrapped in red and silver foil that were used at Maman's only on that night.

"You're crazy to have a dinner for all of us the day after Valentine's night," Midge yelped when she heard of Laine's plans. "You'll be dead!"

"Not this year with Payne helping," Laine assured her. "Besides, that's a special day for friends, and I want to give my thank-you party then." The others, not realizing what was involved, were delighted to accept her invitation to dinner on Sunday.

Laine hired two more of Sam's nieces to help her thoroughly clean her apartment early in the week and threatened Midge with dire counsequences if she messed up anything before Sunday.

Midge kidded Laine about becoming house-proud, but religiously returned the soap to its proper place and dropped her towels in the wicker basket in the bathroom.

Payne, Midge and Laine were in the kitchen early that Saturday morning. Even the lunch crowd expected the heart-shaped petits fours. Spiced apples would be used as a garnish for the kabobs in honor of the holiday.

The big push came after lunch was over and out of the way. The waitresses and Midge quickly changed the tablecloths and placed the sparkling candlesticks on the tables, along with the delicate crystal bowls that each contained a single red rose. Ceramic, red heart-shaped napkin rings held the napkins.

Under Sam's supervision, Gschu and Mei were assembling the individual Salade Jardinières or appetizer trays of tiny pickled beets, marinated beans, carrots with sour cream, thin egg slices with mustard sauce, fish in tarragon butter and stuffed olives. The trays were then outlined in parsley and watercress sprigs with apple slices dipped in red cinnamon syrup.

Payne had the orange sauce for the Duck à l'Orange just at its carmelized stage. The smell of roasting duck permeated the kitchen. The strawberry tarts stood ready on the serving table. The potatoes were being mashed and readied to become sculptured pastry around the slabs of duckling.

The florist had enlivened their day by delivering three boxes from Colin in honor of the special day. Laine received white roses, Midge enjoyed her red ones and Payne was transported by a dozen yellow roses. Emilie called to say that she'd received a dozen pink roses from Colin and a pink box of chocolates that must be a yard wide from Bernie. Bernie had sent Joey an entire month's supply of candy from Jones's, much to Midge's dismay.

"What do you suppose he'll send us?" Midge groaned.

Everything was on simmer and they were about to go up and change for dinner when Bernie's offerings arrived. Laine received a monstrous white satin heart, Midge's was red and Payne's was yellow.

"He did try to get our colors right," Midge said, sighing ruefully, lugging her box upstairs.

"I love it," announced Laine. "You can't overdo on Valentine's Day. I'm not giving this away to our customers either."

"He overdoes everything," Midge moaned.

"You can't be liked too much," Laine said firmly, zipping up her sister's red taffeta dress.

Midge looked at the giant satin hearts and the roses. "It's fun to get Valentine presents again. He even remembered mama and Joey."

They looked in Laine's mirror at the reflection of two girls in red dresses. "We're both Rose Red tonight," Midge smiled.

"Don't forget to wear your red tomorrow to dinner," Laine reminded. "Bernie will love it."

"What about you? Are you going to wear your red silk for Colin?"

"I'm going to wear it for Valentine's Day."

Midge's brown eyes looked into her twin's hazel ones as she spoke hesitantly. "I like Colin, Laine. I really do, but you know he's not like Andy or even Bernie. He's the kind of man who gets his own way."

"So?"

"You're the kind of woman who's always giving and rarely takes."

"I don't know what you're trying to say, Midge."

"I just want you to be sure that you want what Colin wants. I know you've given up an awful lot, and you're just beginning to get some of your own back. Colin is the type of man who just takes over."

"I promise I'll be careful."

"Please, Laine. Love a man who loves you more than himself. You deserve it. He's so self-reliant. He's commanding even when he isn't giving commands. You know what I mean? Oh, forget it. I don't know what I mean."

"I'm not going to get in over my head, Midge. We're just friends."

Midge turned away from Laine. "I don't think he can be friends with you, Laine. I've seen him looking at you when you don't see him. He isn't seeing a friend."

"What do you think he is seeing?" Laine felt uncomfortable.

"Something he's hungered for. Something he wants to possess. Something he's waiting for and is sure he will possess." Midge passed her hand over her eyes. "I'm getting weird in my old age. I shouldn't have skipped lunch. Just take your time with this man, sis."

"No problem. Laine switched off the light as they headed downstairs. A small warning lingered in her mind from her sister's words. Possession wasn't loving. Did Colin know the difference?

Chapter Eight

Payne stayed overnight to help Laine get ready for the Valentine thank-you dinner. "It's really unfair to expect your help when you're one of the people I want to thank." Laine reached past Payne to pick up the napkins she was folding.

She stood back and surveyed her table. The snowy-white cloth with its centerpiece of red roses à la Colin and last night's crystal candlesticks sparkled under the luminous glow of the chandelier she and Colin had discovered at a flea market. Its glass chimneys were etched with the same antique lilies-of-the-valley pattern as her grandmother's crystal.

"It's too bad I had to use restaurant dishes," Laine said, sighing regretfully, "but I didn't have time to hunt up a new set. Mama's blue-and-white stoneware didn't really suit the occasion."

"I'm delighted to be included." Payne inspected the large cake she'd decorated. "It's the best thank-you I could have had. I've never really been part of a family until now."

Laine admired Payne's cake, decorated to resemble an old-fashioned Victorian valentine. Already Payne's cakes were getting a reputation of their own and orders were flooding in for her special designs. "You really are an artist, Payne. It's a shame to eat it."

"You'll never get Bernie and Andy to believe that," Payne replied, giggling. "I'll go start the Cornish hens while you dress."

"Oh no you won't," Laine admonished. "We'll both get ready and we'll both go down together."

Payne's dress was white wool adorned with a ruby pin in the shape of two hearts. She'd let Laine pull her fine hair up into an elaborate twist that gave the long face a partrician look and accentuated the wide gray eyes.

"Heavens, I look positively sophisticated." Payne stared at herself wonderingly in the glass.

Laine's red dress rustled over its taffeta petticoat. "I love your dress. It looks as though it came straight from France."

"It did," Payne admitted.

Ignoring Shadow's demanding meows from the study where he'd been incarcerated for Emilie's sake, they went down to prepare the meal. After the Cornish hens were glazed and stuffed with the wild-rice dressing, they were gently slid into the oven. Laine made the excuse that she'd forgotten something and left Payne to coat the chantilly potatoes with their cream mixture while she ran upstairs.

Deftly she pulled out a shopping bag full of the red and white wrapped packages she'd accumulated during the past few weeks and set one at each place. The name tags on each gift would serve as a place card. She paused to admire the charming table one more time, then whisked downstairs. She was just in time to fold the grated cheese into the Corn Creole. The asparagus and the peas wouldn't be cooked until the last minute in order to keep their flavor fresh.

"Why both?" Payne inquired, brushing butter on top of the dinner rolls.

"Joey and Bernie won't touch asparagus, but it's my mother's favorite." Laine set the cut-glass relish dish out ready to fill with appetizers. The salads were already in the upstairs refrigerator, waiting for their chiffonade dressing.

Payne sat down and admired the hors d'oeuvre table that Laine had set up. "Everything is so pretty, Laine. I'm glad you're putting the hors d'oeuvres down here so that we can talk to our friends while we finish the cooking."

"Did you think we'd be working down here while they enjoyed themselves upstairs? I suppose I could have hired one of the girls to serve today while we played ladies of leisure, but I really prefer to do my own serving for friends."

"Me, too!" Payne got up to help carry the trays of appetizers to the table. "I love stuffed brussel sprouts. I could eat my whole meal right here."

"You'd better now," Laine warned her. "Hors d'oeuvres are supposed to pique the appetite, not kill it." She looked over the stuffed celery and cucumber lillies. "Those were the first things my grandmother taught me to make." They put the trays and dishes of delicacies around the centerpiece Payne had created out of red velvet hearts and white lace with sweetheart roses peeking out of baby's breath bouquets. By the time the punch bowl was filled, the guests were arriving.

Andy wafted in, lured by the enticing aroma of baking Cornish hens. He presented the women with pencil-and-pad sets decorated with red hearts. Payne was delighted with hers and promised to use them for all her notes. Andy put Midge's on the table and snatched a few olives to tide him over. Bernie came in accompanied by Emilie, Midge and Joey. While Joey tore upstairs to visit Shadow, the Marshields arrived with a set of blue-and-white jars for Laine's kitchen.

"We thought it might as well be a housewarming, too." They put their jars beside another of Bernie's mammonth satin hearts. This one was rainbow satin topped with a gigantic bouquet of plastic flowers.

"I thought you might've given all the candy from yesterday to your customers," he defended himself.

When Laine straightened up from basting the poultry, Colin was beside her. "You look very appetizing yourself in that red dress," he commented. "I can hardly wait to see it when you unwrap yourself." Laine and Payne had protected their dresses with large white chef's aprons.

"Get ready," Laine laughed. "We're about to unwrap." While everyone feasted on appetizers, Midge showed Emilie around the apartment. Laine sent Bernie, Andy and Colin upstairs with the serving dishes, entrusting the hens to Frank. She, Midge and Payne quickly covered the perishables and tucked them away before following the others upstairs.

Her guests decided not to open their gifts until after dinner, Joey being the only objector. One look from Midge silenced him. Laine had to laugh because Midge reminded her of their mother when she'd silenced the youthful twins with the same look.

The dinner was a huge success. Laine and Payne gathered enough compliments to satisfy an army of chefs.

They complimented each other on their mutual work until Joey interrupted them disgustedly with a reminder about the unopened gifts. Since he was on Laine's left, Joey went first. Gleefully he opened the familiar Jones's box of special valentine treats. Midge moaned loudly at the other end of the table when she saw the taffy sticks, but gave Joey permission to leave and show his loot to Shadow. He carefully excused himself, picked up a napkin full of scraps he'd saved for the cat and disappeared. Payne was next. Opening the long jewelry box, she found a bracelet with one charm, a small gold frying pan with a garnet heart set inside it. "Oh, Laine. It's a symbol of a chef with my birthstone on it. Thank you!"

Andy looked at his similar box suspiciously. "Do you think the students will appreciate my charm bracelet?" As the group laughed, he opened the box to find a silver letter opener. He read the engraving out loud. "'The law is the last result of human wisdom.'" His voice had a gruff sound. "Thank you, Laine. I've always appreciated Samuel Johnson. I've quoted that to my students every year. 'The law is the last result of human wisdom setting upon human experience for the benefit of the public.' It's everything a law instructor tries to teach. Thank you."

Joy admired her bracelet with the tiny silver bootee on it. "I'll add a charm for every important event in the baby's life. It's a wonderful gift!"

Frank was enchanted by the carved wooden box made especially to hold his business cards. Laine had commissioned it from a wood-carver in the university village. The Marshields' names were carved on it, along with the name of the shop. "Now people can take a card without knocking the whole pile on the floor. It's beautiful work,

Laine. You know how much I appreciate handmade work!"

Midge did cry about her bracelet with the tiny computer and a sapphire heart. She knew that it represented Laine's good wishes for her in her new endeavour. She was still mopping her eyes with Bernie's handkerchief when he opened his gift.

It was a tiny tool-set of precision instruments made for detailed miniature work. Bernie had often complained about how hard it was to get tools for some of his microcomputer work. He touched each small instrument with the delicacy of a surgeon and regaled them with all of the things he was going to create with them. His gratitude was overwhelming and made Laine feel very humble.

Emilie smiled at her own gift of a heart with her birthstone surrounded by the two sapphires of the twins and Joey's emerald.

"They're only chips, mama," Laine assured her. "Someday we'll get the real thing."

Laine watched Colin open his gift with some trepidation. She'd found it at the university bookstore in a section reserved for the sale of student work. The piece she'd chosen had been sculpted from wood by a graduate art student. It had reminded her of her conversation with Colin the Sunday morning they'd talked of his childhood. He looked at her curiously as he folded back the paper from the ten-inch-high statue. He stared at it in complete silence. The others looked at the piece and each other. Laine had the sinking feeling that she'd failed to communicate with this particular gift.

It was the figure of a young man rising from a formless mass of rough-hewed wood. One hand pushed down the grasping prison while the other hand was raised to the heavens. The head was thrown back in determination, and the cords of the neck stood out in the struggle to overcome the heavy wood trying to bind the man to the ground. His eyes were fixed on a goal above. It was a testimony to the incredible endurance and strength of the human spirit. It was entitled *Victory* in carving across the base.

Laine was chilled by the absolute lack of expression on Colin's face. She cleared her throat to try and explain, realizing that what was beauty to one person might not be to another.

"It was the title." She looked hopefully at the rest of the group. "Colin means victory. That's the title of the sculpture."

The others started chattering. They vociferously admired the piece, saying how appropriate, attractive or interesting the art object was. Colin still sat staring silently at the statue. As the nervous chatter died down, he turned and focused on Laine. She was glad to see that his eyes were alive again.

"This is a result of our Sunday-morning conversation I take it. It's very moving, Laine. I can honestly say that no gift has ever pleased me more. Thank you."

"You scared us for a minute there, buddy," Bernie blurted out. "I thought from your expresson that you were mad or something. I don't know much about art, but that looks pretty good to me."

"I was affected by the sculpture, Bernie," Colin answered evenly.

"Couldn't you be affected with a smile?" Bernie grated. "We thought you were going to bawl Laine out."

Laine stopped Bernie from pursuing the subject by offering the cake as a sacrifice. Bernie was more than happy to be sidetracked by chocolate cake and the conversation slipped into safer channels.

"I can't believe I ate that enormous piece of cake on top of such a large meal." Joy staggered from the table to the living room. "This baby is going to be born with a terrible lust for French cooking that I'll never be able to satisfy."

"I can see the kid now," Frank joked, "hanging around Maman's alley door, waiting for handouts from Laine and Payne to feed his habit."

"Why not?" Andy countered. "I do it all the time. He won't have to stand out in the alley. The girls will invite him in. They take pity on everyone."

Bernie lumbered in with a handful of dishes. "Come on, you guys, we'll let the women rest while we put these in the dishwasher downstairs. Up and at 'em!" Laine rescued the crystal, but let Bernie and the men take the dishes down to the kitchen. She and Midge quickly washed the glasses and put them away. Payne and Joy stuffed leftovers into the refrigerator while Joey ate his cake and returned to his furry gray playmate.

Emilie touched the crisp gingham curtains. "It's so pleasant now. You and your friends have done wonders, *chérie*. This is a much nicer place for you to live. Maurice always preferred the darker colors and the older ways, but this is much better for you."

"I'm glad you like it, maman." Laine hugged Emilie. "Maybe you'll come and visit me often."

"My room is très elegant," Emilie pronounced. "It was thoughtful of you, Madelaine." Her glance caught the *Victory* sculpture on the table in the dining room. "That's a beautiful thing, daughter."

"Yes, I thought so. I'm only sorry Colin didn't like it as much as I thought he would. He's done so much for me in these past weeks. I wanted to thank him with something special."

Emilie looked at her daughter shrewdly. "But you did."

"He certainly didn't seem very impressed." Laine looked downcast.

Emilie put her hands on either side of Laine's face. "Madelaine, are you sure you understand the kind of man Colin Laird is? He's not a man who shows his emotions easily. He's the kind of man who feels the most when he shows it the least. The sculpture struck him in the heart. I know. Your father was much like him in his ways. They make a big show of showing nothing."

"He certainly did that."

"Are you serious about this man, Madelaine?" Emilie's brown eyes were intent. "If you're not, don't encourage him."

"What is it you and Midge are afraid of in Colin?" Laine asked. "She warned me he might be too possessive and now you seem to be concerned."

"I like him and so does Midge." Emilie looked at the statue reflectively. "You were perceptive in your gift. "He's much like the subject in the sculpture. He's won his own soul over great odds. He's used to victory, but he isn't one to give his heart away easily. Once given, he might be unwilling or unable to give the object of his love room to breathe. I sense a deep need in him. Are you willing to make that need your own?"

"I don't know, mama." Laine patted her mother's hand comfortingly. "Don't worry. We're only friends at the moment."

"Oh no, my dear. When you gave him that particular gift, you passed over the boundaries of friendship into something else. That's how Colin saw it. That's how all your friends perceived it. You're no longer just friends. You're not a child to believe that foolishness. You're a woman, and you made a public commitment of some kind with this gift. Surely you're aware of this?"

Laine thought for a moment and answered honestly. "Yes. It wasn't clear at the time I bought the gift, but I think I knew it when I gave it to him."

Emilie squeezed Laine's hand. "It's only because we love you that we nag you so much, Laine. You've given so much to us. We want you to have all that you deserve."

"Do you think Bernie and Midge will get together?" Laine changed the subject.

Emilie's eyes twinkled. "I think Midge can't resist all of that raw material to make something of. Mignon was ever one to take up the underdog. I think Bernie knows this as well as we do and plays up to it. Joey is very fond of him. Bernie's patient and will wait for her to make up her mind. They share many interests and though his manners are common, his heart is not. He's what you call a diamond in the rough, I think. When Midge is finished, he'll be a diamond in its proper setting."

Midge came up behind them. "What makes you two think I'm interested in polishing up such a rough diamond?"

"You can't help yourself," Laine quipped. "Besides, Bernie is a sucker for big brown eyes; namely, yours, mama's and Joey's."

"He can fall in love with a mirror then," Midge retorted. "His own eyes are a deeper brown than ours."

"Ah, she noticed." Emilie lifted an eyebrow with amusement.

"Hmm. I fell for that one," Midge admitted, and went to greet the men who were returning from their kitchen duty. Colin and Bernie brought up in the rear carrying a fish tank and a large grocery bag.

"This is Torvald Turtle," Colin explained, putting the large tank on the dining-room table. "He's Joey's new pet."

"Isn't he a rather large turtle?" Midge muttered.

"He's a box turtle. The little ones are more prone to problems than the larger land turtles. Torvald is already eight years old and used to humans. He belonged to a friend who's moving to Germany this month with the air force, so he needed a new owner. They can live to be around forty or so."

Bernie informed Joey of Torvald's arrival so the rest of the afternoon passed watching Torvald's antics.

"I had no idea turtles were so outgoing." Joy watched Torvald rumble across the rug to investigate Bernie's foot. Joey followed him, enchanted by his new pet. "I thought they'd be slimy, more like a reptile. His little paw, or claw, or whatever is perfectly dry."

"I'm glad we've never made a habit of serving turtle soup," Midge jested.

"Mooother," Joey yelped.

"I'm sure I'll get uesd to him in time." Midge tried to be philosophical. "He has such beady little eyes."

"He loves to watch TV," Colin informed Joey. "My friend said that he was particularly fond of video games."

"A smart turtle." Bernie picked up the creature. "He'll fit right in."

"Speaking of beady eyes," Emilie said, smiling, "it's time for old folk, little folk and turtles to go home and get ready for school tomorrow."

Everyone trooped downstairs to say goodbye to Bernie and company. Joy and Frank thanked Laine again for their gifts and a wonderful day as they unlocked their door. Andy swung Payne's overnight bag to his shoulder and walked her to the parking lot where his car awaited them.

Colin was standing behind Laine as she waved Payne and Andy into the cloud of fog that greeted the dusk. He laid her coat across her shoulders. "Let's go for a walk, my lady, and work off some of that dinner."

Laine reached for the key hanging inside the door, and he put on his own coat as she locked up. He helped her slip into her coat, letting his fingers linger tantalizingly on her throat. She could feel her heart pounding and wondered if he realized he was responsible for the rapid pulse.

The fog had crept into the alley and surrounded them. His lips were close to her ear and his whisper mesmerized her.

"Madelaine, it was a lovely day, but I thought I'd never have the chance to be alone with you." Slowly he turned her around, so that she was held against him and she could feel his heart beating nearly as fast as her own. "I brought you outside for your own sake because it would be too much to ask of me to keep my hands off you in the apartment. Do you have any idea how tempting you look in that red dress? Being around you today was a form of refined torture."

Her voice was muffled against his chest. "I thought you were disappointed by the statue. I wanted to show you that I cared."

She felt him tremble briefly. "It struck me dumb. Looking at it was like talking to you. I didn't want to share it."

"I'm sorry." Laine burrowed into his chest.

"I'm not." He tipped her head up and kissed her thoroughly. "I'm only sorry I couldn't thank you the way I wanted to at the time."

"Oh?"

"I'm not used to sharing all my feelings with the world as you seem to be."

"Oh."

"In fact, I'm not used to sharing at all."

"Hmm."

"You're interfering with my work."

"Umm?"

"I keep seeing your face instead of the notes I'm compiling about Jericho and the Jordan Valley. My book on ancient civilizations is suffering from a modern disease."

"What disease is that?" Laine looked up into his eyes.

His arms tightened around her, but he couldn't bring himself to say the words. Instead he tried to make a joke of it. "Madelainitis. It's a serious, disabling complaint that cripples the mind."

"What are the symptoms?"

"Too numerous to list, but I know what the cure is." He took her in his arms and kissed her deeply. "You might take me in and provide some physical therapy."

Why can't he say the word love, Laine thought to herself, but aloud she said, "Let's walk. It'll be good therapy for both of us."

He tucked her arm through his with resignation as they headed down the alley. "That's what I thought you'd say."

They walked toward the university campus and ended up in the quadrant facing the cathedral entrance to the library. Laine grinned teasingly.

"This must be your favorite place."

They sat on one of the stone benches. The fog shimmered and swirled in the lights from the lampposts and eddied around their feet. "Not really." He stroked the palm of her hand with his thumb. "I spent last summer on the Jericho site. It's wild, beautiful country in the

Jordan Valley. You've got the river, the Dead Sea and the mountains. It's set on an oasis, you know. The ancient spring is still providing the irrigation to modern Jericho. Don't you have any desire to see other places in other lands, Laine?"

"Of course I do. My second minor was history in college. I thought I'd be training in Europe then, but all Christians have a fascination with the Holy Land."

"In another year I plan to tour the Orient. Wouldn't you like to indulge yourself in rare Chinese, Japanese or Indian dishes? I'd love to see you in a Chinese silk. They make a color that's the exact shade of your hair. It's a honey color that's shot with threads of shimmering gold." He touched her hair and pulled a strand of it between his fingers as a merchant would finger a fine piece of silk.

"You'd be more apt to find me in the kitchen than wandering around in silks and satins," Laine observed honestly. "I'd love to know the real secrets of Indian curry."

His hand stilled on her hair. "Has anyone told you that you're not exactly the soul of romance, Madelaine Morgan? I've lured you to a particularly romantic place. My students have assured me that their girls love foggy nights in this setting. I've whispered sweet nothings in your ears, and what do I get for my pains? You discuss the possibilities of wresting some poor Indian cook's recipes from him. It's a severe blow to my male ego."

Laine rose and tugged at his hand until he stood beside her. "I want you to like me for what I am, Colin. I don't want you to think of me as some kind of odalisque in Oriental draperies floating through your life. Aren't you trying to think of me in the same way your father thought about your mother? I'm a real woman who lives in a real world and loves to do real things. If that's not what you want, than I'm not what you want."

"What brought this on?" Colin winced.

"I don't know." Laine was confused herself. "I rejected Andy's proposal because he didn't believe in romance. Now I've hurt your feelings because it all seemed a little fake tonight. I'm not making sense even to myself."

"Andy had the nerve to propose?" Colin asked through gritted teeth.

"He's proposed every winter for years," Laine answered absently.

"How dull for you having to refuse a proposal every year." Colin's voice took on a nasty note that Laine could no longer ignore.

"He's lonely and was willing to accept comfort for loving, but I think that Payne will change his mind. She really needs his kind of protection, and he needs someone like Payne who'd concentrate only on him and his desires."

"Do you always find someone else for the men you've rejected?"

"Colin, please don't get upset."

"I'm not upset. Why should I be upset because the woman I've been trying to make love to is planning menus for tomorrow while I kiss her? Why would I be upset about so small a matter?"

"That's not true!"

He started walking briskly toward the way they'd come, dragging Laine along with him. "I don't think you're like my mother. She was a vague, pathetic person who was the shadow of a selfish monomaniac. You're neither vague nor pathetic. If anything, you're opinionated and entirely too independent. I certainly don't see myself as an unapproachable mogul whose only passion is acquiring wealth. If you were a man, Laine, I'd have decked you on the spot for comparing me to my father. I think you suffer from a severe case of reverse snobbery. You're so stiff-necked about being a working woman, you've stopped being a woman. You act like one and you certainly look like one, but one to one with a man, you run like a scared rabbit and hide under a camouflage of duty and family. I wonder if you'd have loved a man even if all of your family problems had never happened."

Laine dug in her feet and jolted both of them to a standstill. "Colin, I'm not one of your students and you won't reduce me to a jellyfish with those kinds of accusations. You talk about trips to China and the Orient. You try to make love to me. What makes you different from Andy? He honestly admitted that he wasn't in love. You never once said anything about loving me or caring about anything except what I look like. You were treating me as a thing, the same way you'd treat an interesting artifact you found on one of your trips. You'd dress me like a doll and put me in romantic settings like a work of art. I'm a human being, not an acquisition. You can't acquire me without my consent. You're arrogant, Colin Laird! I haven't demanded that you change. I accept the way you dress, talk and live. Why do you attack my outlook?"

"You need changing," Colin muttered tightly.

"Perhaps we both do," Laine retorted. "You may be right about my being afraid of a relationship with a man. But what is it that makes me afraid?"

"How would I know. Maybe you have some kind of hang up!"

"Yes. I want to love a man who loves me for what I am. I'd love him for himself. I won't marry him to change him, and I don't want to be changed by marriage. Loving should add to people's lives, not take away from them."

"Love is always a compromise. Someone has to give in." Colin's face was averted from hers.

"Oh, Colin. That's not true. Giving isn't always giving in. You can't base the idea of loving on what you experienced with your parents. They were very sad."

Colin turned and faced her with a cold, deadly gaze. "Why, then that must make me sad, too, doesn't it?"

They walked home in utter silence because they were both too hurt to speak. Laine felt that she'd never break through the wall of anger that surrounded him, and her heart lay like a stone inside her breast. He left her at the door without a word. Waiting for her on her new table was the statue of Victory. For the first time since her father's death, Laine was racked by deep sobs.

Chapter Nine

Laine didn't see Colin for the next two weeks and friends carefully avoided mentioning their estrangement. Bernie reported to Midge that Colin had buried himself on the houseboat in a "pile of books and notes about ancient cities" and saw no one. He didn't tell her that he'd tried to talk to Colin about Laine and had been severely put down. Bernie took Midge and Laine to dinner at other restaurants while Payne held down the fort at Maman's.

Joy and Frank found items for the apartment at low prices and walked to church with Laine on Sundays. Emilie wisely didn't introduce the subject and merely discussed safe family topics.

Payne was a wonderful addition to Maman's and to Laine's life. She was a brilliant cook and rapidly learned the recipes used in the restaurant. Her eagerness and her very real talent helped fill Laine's days with a sense of accomplishment. The nights were a different matter, and she couldn't hide the dark circles under her eyes with any amount of makeup artistry.

"She misses him so much," Joy confided to Frank. "They seemed so perfect for each other. I can't imagine what could have gone wrong."

"Sometimes kindred spirits are not kindred hearts, little one," Frank said as he kissed her curly head. "Often people who seem perfectly matched physically, socially and mentally don't always see eye to eye emotionally."

"I guess we're kindred hearts and not kindred minds," she teased. "It's the heart that counts."

He laid his hand on her blossoming tummy. "Always."

Midge was all for going down to the houseboat and bearding the lion in his watery den. Bernie restrained her.

"I know him. You don't force Colin to do anything."

"I just want to ask him why he walked out on Laine," Midge explained.

"Hey, Midge. They weren't married. They could walk out on each other any time if they wanted to. How do you know she didn't walk out on him?"

Midge looked at him in disgust. "Do you see any dark circles under his eyes?"

"Yeah, as a matter of fact I do," Bernie said.

"Really?"

"Yeah."

Midge sat on the sofa and asked thoughtfully, "Bernie, did you try to talk to him?"

"I did and got my head bitten off in a polite way."

"I can't imagine what could have happened." Midge leaned back into Bernie' grateful arms. "How could he possibly be mad at Laine?"

"Maybe he's not mad. Maybe he's just hurt." Bernie was entranced by the soft hair against his cheek. "Maybe he thinks that Laine doesn't love him."

Midge looked up at Bernie in amazement. "How could he believe that after the statue she gave him? We all saw how she looked at him. Is he blind?"

"We men appreciate being told we're liked too, you know." Bernie looked pained. "Sometimes we feel like we're just something to escort you to the movies, send flowers or open doors. Maybe Laine made Colin think that she didn't care. I know the feeling. Sometimes you forget I have any feelings. I'm different from Colin. I hang in there, but Colin is more sensitive than I am."

Midge looked at the big square hand covering hers. She remembered the days before Bernie when the evenings were too long and the days dreary. She thought of Joey's happiness at being included by Bernie in many of their activities. Bernie had calmed down a great deal since that first night in the kitchen of Maman's. He'd become a warm and important part of her family life. It happened so naturally that Midge hadn't even been aware of how he'd fit into her world. Suddenly she thought of what her life would be like without the great kindly bear sitting next to her. She shivered and he tightened his hold.

"What's wrong?"

Midge patted his hand. "I was thinking that I haven't thanked you for all that you've done for Joey and me."

"Forget it."

"No, Bernie. I don't want to forget it." She lifted her face to his.

After a pause while Bernie digested her meaning, he leaned forward and kissed her. "Midge, you know I love you and Joey. Will you both marry me?"

"Why else would I get you to buy that new blue suit," Midge asked mistily.

"Huh?"

"Yes, Bernie. I'll marry you. Joey would never forgive me if I didn't."

"What about you?"

"I wouldn't forgive me if I didn't, either."

Much later Midge informed Bernie about an idea she'd just formed. He looked unsure of the situation, but agreed to go along with the plan.

Monday, with Payne's help, Midge kidnapped Laine and took her shopping. When Laine tried on a soft dress of brown and amber tweed, Midge not only made her sister buy it, but they snipped off the tags and Laine wore it out of the shop.

"You need cheering up and you look smashing in that dress. It brings out those amber flecks in your eyes," Midge commanded, steering Laine into a shop that was showing some new makeup lines for the coming spring.

Laine ended up with a cherry-bronze lipstick and an eye shadow called green sapphire. She went to the hairdressers to wait for Midge, who was getting a feathery new cut and let them talk her into having her hair washed and blow-dried so that it fell to her shoulders in a sheet of tawny silk.

Laine completely missed the conspiring looks between the beautician and her sister as they pretended that this spontaneous event had just happened because someone had cancelled. Actually, Midge had made their appointments days earlier.

"We'll drop the car off at Bernie's so he can take us home." Midge headed toward the lake and Bernie's houseboat. She was well satisfied with her part of the plan and trusted Bernie completely to perform his part.

They parked the car to be greeted by an apparently empty boat.

"Where on earth could he be?" Midge looked elaborately bewildered.. "Oh, here's a note stuck to the cabin door. 'Midge, can you pick me up at the university? Ask Laine to please stay as I'm expecting an important package. Sorry about the mix-up. Love, Bernie.'"

"Isn't that typical?" Midge didn't quite meet Laine's eyes. "I'll rush over and get him and be right back. Do you mind waiting for the package?" Midge unlocked the cabin door with the keys on Bernie's chain.

Laine agreed to stay. "I've always wanted to see the inside of Bernie's boat anyway." Midge rushed off, leaving Laine to admire the interior of the houseboat. It was neat and tidy like Bernie himself.

Once she got used to the hum of the generator and the gentle rocking under her feet, Laine could see it's appeal as a perfect bachelor quarters. The immaculate galley with its built-in breakfast nook was absolutely shipshape. Laine decided Bernie and Midge might like some coffee when they returned, so she plugged in the pot and filled it with coffee from the canister on the counter. The stove was small but had a little oven and broiler perfect for one or two servings. It would be a challenge to cook creatively on this, Laine thought as she hunted up some mugs with the logo of a local gas station printed on them.

A desk in the living-room section testified to Bernie's latest electronic project. A neat pile of corrected math papers showed that he was keeping up with his students' work at the university. Laine sank into Bernie's deep, comfortable chair and thought about how this friendly, compact home combined the easy comfort and working accuracy that was Bernie. Everything was well-worn and shabby, except the tools of his various trades and hobbies. Midge said that when he taught, he was extremely meticulous and educated in his language. It was only when he was just another person in the group that his language reverted to his origins. Bernie was an interesting dichotomy, much like the old coffee can full of plastic spoons sitting next to the shiny, dustless case of precision tools.

A knock on the cabin door interrupted her thoughts. Thinking that it must be Bernie's package, she opened it expecting to see a delivery man. It was a package, but it was being delivered by Colin Laird.

"Hi, Laine." A certain tenseness around the jawline was the only sign that her presence was a surprise. "Bernie asked me to bring this over at eight."

"He's not here yet. I'm expecting him soon. Midge went to pick him up. We borrowed his car for a shopping trip." Laine knew she was talking too much and too fast but couldn't seem to stop because he made her so nervous.

"Well, will you give him this? He said it was essential that he have it by eight."

"He was probably held up at the university."

They stood looking at each other helplessly.

"Well, I have a great deal of work to do." Colin handed her the package.

"Don't go, Colin," Laine begged. "I've just made some coffee. Would you like some?"

His face was totally shuttered. It's as though I was a stranger, Laine thought with dismay. Then she remembered what her mother had said about men like Colin showing the least what they felt the most. Impulsively she reached out and took his hand.

"Oh, please come in, Colin. I'm sorry I hurt you. Can't we be friends again?"

His eyes were like smoked-amber glass that reflected no light as he pulled his hand away from hers. "Madelaine, don't mistake hurting for irritating. You have something I wanted. You weren't willing to give it. Our relationship hadn't progressed far enough for hurting." He turned to leave.

Laine took a deep breath as she saw his retreating back. "I'm sorry to hear that, because you hurt me and I'm still bleeding from the wounds." She saw his back stiffen at her words and he paused on the deck of the boat.

"I apologize." Colin's voice was a monotone. He stepped off the deck onto the dock and walked over to the next boat. Not once did he turn and look her way.

When Midge and Bernie returned, they found Laine sitting, her eyes lifeless, staring blindly out onto the lake from the galley porthole. A cold cup of coffee untouched on the table before her.

Bernie shrugged helplessly. "I told you it wouldn't work. Colin is too proud to be maneuvered. He must have seen through your plan."

Midge slid into the booth across from Laine. "Didn't he even stop for coffee?"

Laine looked dully back at Midge. "He didn't stop at all."

Bernie crowded in beside Midge. "Well, I know it's not another woman or anything like that. He gets plenty of chances with all of the meetings he goes to. There's an English instructor who's been chasing him for weeks. I'd know if there were any women around on the boat. He went up to his place on Port Townsend last weekend. It couldn't have been too much fun because it's cold up there now. He doesn't usually open it until May or June.

It's an old Victorian house and isn't set up for anything except summer heating."

Midge hesitated and then blurted out her question. "Laine, maybe we could help if we knew what actually happened?"

"Don't tell us if you don't want to," Bernie hastened to add.

Laine gave the two dear faces a lopsided grin that made them feel worse than if she had wept. "It wasn't that serious. At least I didn't think it was." She proceeded to tell them the details of that night, omitting only the kisses.

"It must have been comparing him to his father," Bernie stated at the end of her narration. "Above all things, he doesn't want to be the kind of man his father was. He has a real thing about it. That man must have been a cross between Nero and Machiavelli."

"Payne said that Colin's father was an absolute tyrant. The mother had no spirit of her own. He was always taunting her with the fact that she couldn't have any more children after Colin was born as though it were deliberate misbehavior on her part. I guess Colin fought his father all his life. Payne said they never had yelling fights. They were much worse because they were cold deadly duels between two expert swordsmen. Desmond Laird used ridicule and humiliation to hurt Colin. Colin treated his father with a kind of icy contempt. Payne said it used to give her the willies when they were in the same room," Midge offered.

"I accused him of being like his father," Laine murmured miserably.

"I think if you'd been me, he'd have knocked you down," Bernie volunteered.

"That's what he said," Laine confirmed thoughtfully. "I think you're right, Bernie. I pushed a button I didn't mean to."

"Still, he should be sensible," Midge argued. "He was doing the same number on you, wasn't he? It seems to me that you're doing all the giving in this relationship."

"What about all of his work and time on the apartment?" Bernie defeneded his friend stoutly.

"Bernie," Midge said nailing him, "suppose I said that I'd love you only if you gave up all of your electronic stuff and followed me into the company next fall when I take my new job. I might promise you money and all the luxuries you could want, but you'd have to give up your inventing and your teaching because it didn't fit in with my life-style?"

"You wouldn't do that to me." Bernie was horrified.

"Of course I wouldn't, silly." Midge patted his hand. "Would you tell me to give up my new job after I spent four years training for it because you didn't want me to work?"

"Not if you didn't want to," Bernie admitted. "But I'm not Colin." He fooled with his coffee cup unhappily. "I know you think he's being unreasonable, Midge, but none of us can escape our pasts. I'll always come from Hell's Kitchen. You might get me to speak decent English and fold my napkin right, but you'll never be able to take those years out of my life or my personality. I was a tough little kid in a tough world. I'm out of it now, because of my education and a knack with salable products. But it'll always be there."

Midge kissed him. "I like tough little kids."

He put his arm around her. "Colin came from a tough place, too. I didn't have his money, but I didn't have to face an enemy in my own home, either."

Laine's aching heart warmed at the affection between Bernie and Midge. She said as much to them.

Bernie looked at her warmly. "I never had a sister. I'm looking forward to it, Laine. Hang in there. Colin's a really good man. Maybe he seems unreasonable to you girls. I only see that he wanted someone to love him more than they loved their work. He got the idea that Laine didn't and it hurt him. I know he said he wasn't hurt. He lied; he was hurt. I'm a man and I know when a guy is suffering. If you really care about him, Laine, you've got to go tell him. If you don't care, leave him alone so that he can heal himself. He's not the kind of man you can fool with."

"You aren't accusing Laine of being a tease, are you?" Midge inquired bristling.

Bernie looked at Laine compassionately. "I think Laine has worked so hard to do what she's done that she wasn't ready for someone like Colin. Midge is different from you, Laine. She's the kind of woman who needs the whole thing; a home, a family and interesting work. If the laundry doesn't get done, it won't bother Midge. She won't feel bad if we eat TV dinners occasionally. She'll be able to leave her work at the office and come home to me and Joey." He shifted uncomfortably.

"Laine, you're an all or nothing person. You'd stay up all night to do the laundry and then work a full day. You didn't touch the apartment until it could be exactly the way you wanted it. You're willing to work too many hours to make a success of your job. You're awfully hard on yourself and sometimes that makes it hard to come up to your standards. I know I couldn't. Andy couldn't. You have to have a man as good at what he does as you are at what you do—"

"Bernie," Laine interrupted, "I want a home and family just like Midge."

"But you're an idealist, " Bernie explained. "You want perfection. You're waiting for the perfect man to be dropped into your lap, Laine. I don't know anyone who is handsome, successful, sensitive and a restauranteur to boot."

"That's not fair!" Midge pulled her hand away from Bernie's.

"Yes, it is," Laine acknowledged. "I've been guilty of expecting perfection in everything. Bernie didn't mean I was a tease. He meant that I was a coward. I won't take chances on another person. I've been as selfish about Colin as I was about Midge. I expected both of them to be what I wanted rather than what they were. I wasn't playing fair. It wasn't deliberate, I was just walking around with blinders on. I can see where that would look like leading a man on. Maybe I couldn't make up my mind about Colin because I wasn't looking for love, I was looking for a perfect male who doesn't exist."

"I don't remember saying all that." Bernie smiled with relief.

"You're being too hard on yourself as usual," Midge insisted loyally.

"No." Laine got up and started for the door. "I was being too hard on Colin. He has every right to be angry with me."

"Wait a minute! Let's not go overboard," Bernie protested.

"But that's exactly what I'm going to do." Laine waved as she exited.

She jumped off Bernie's boat to the dock and then walked the few steps to Colin's boat and stepped onto its deck. When she looked through the porthole in the door, she saw him sitting at a desk with his head in his hands. He looked so forlorn that her heart caught in her throat.

Knowing how much he'd hate having her see him like that, Laine quietly retraced her steps to the dock. She managed to make considerable noise coming across the gangplank this time, which wasn't easy with size-five shoes. By the time she made it to the door, he was waiting on the other side.

"You'd better let me in, Colin Laird," Laine threatened to the door. "I can stand out here and scream horrible things in French for four hours and embarrass you before all the other faculty members on the boats. I can see two people peeking out of their portholes right this minute!"

He opened the door. "In," he commanded, hauling her through the door.

Laine looked up into his tired eyes and her courage almost failed her. She squared her shoulders and let fly. "Colin Laird, I love you even if you don't love me. I love you more than my restaurant. I even love you more than my beautiful new apartment. I love you more than my family or my pride. I was hurt the other night because you never once said you even cared for me, but I'd rather have your liking than anyone else's loving. Now, will you forgive me?"

He pulled her into his arms and buried his face in her hair. "I missed you."

"I'm not exactly a moving target, Colin. You could have contacted me any time in the past two weeks." His soft brown sweater smelled like some kind of woody soap, a scent she associated only with him.

"You should have known that my intentions were honorable."

"How? You warned me over and over that they were dishonorable." She pulled back to look up at him. "Are you telling me to go away again? Is this a polite brush off?"

His mouth came down on hers in a kiss that was fierce, demanding and hungry. The savagery of that kiss reminded Laine not to tease a sleeping lion. He picked her up and deposited her on his lap as he sat down in a leather armchair. Only when she was in danger of suffocation did he release her lips.

"If you go away from me again," he growled, "it will be your choice, not mine."

"Could we possibly get to know each other a little bettter?" Laine ran her fingers through the crisp hairs at the nape of his neck. "We might even like each other when we're not fighting. I've more time now that Payne is doing so well. You were right when you said I was afraid of men. I'm afraid of having my life taken over. Will you give me a chance to get used to the idea?"

"Funny, I could have sworn you were reacting positively a minute ago." He looked down into her eyes and she bloomed under the warmth of his gaze.

"Oh, Colin, you know that I love you. But that's an easy trap to fall into. You're extremely attractive. I'm only saying a lifetime can't be spent making love. What if I turn out to be allergic to Oriental food or get seasick when you're writing a book on the Venice Canals? I might be a terrible drag on you. What about children? What about our beliefs, our outlooks and our cats?"

He threw back his head and laughed until she joined him. She noticed that the lines around his eyes had smoothed out and softened. He gave her one of his familiar wicked looks.

"You'd better get off my lap if you want a real courtship, Madelaine. The temptation to make it the shortest courtship in history would be too strong if you stay where you are."

She brushed his mouth with hers as she extricated herself from his arms. Even though she desired above all things to remain where she was, she recognized the wisdom of his statement.

Smiling at her, he went to open the door into the corridor leading to the bedrooms. Two brown cats leaped out meowing loudly, obviously bawling him out for having locked them away. "I can take care of the cat problem right away. Meet Odd and Essey, my two Burmese. I lock them away because they want to lie on my notes and play. I was working on my Greek book when a friend gave them to me. I happened to be doing Homer's *Odyssey*. They'd journeyed throughout the states with him, but he was leaving for a dig in Egypt. He couldn't take them, so they ended their odyssey with me."

Odd meowed inquiringly and sniffed at Laine's ankles. She promptly threw herself at Laine's feet in a heap. Essey ran to her twin and fell on top of her. Laine picked up one in each arm and retired to the leather armchair where they settled in her lap with throbbing purrs.

"You can see they're very hard to get along with," Colin joked. "They've an absolutely uncritical love of human beings. They get along with other cats as well if you were thinking about Shadow. Besides, he's a male so there would be no competition."

Laine stopped petting Odd for a moment only to have the cat hook a paw around her wrist to remind her to continue. She laughed at the antics of the brown cats. Colin smiled at her in delight.

"They're called the clowns of the cat world. You can see why."

"Laine!" Midge's concerned voice came through the door as a heavy knock announced Bernie's presence. Colin looked a trifle irritated but unsurprised.

"Your protectors have come to see if you're alive and unharmed."

Midge knew at a glance that all was well and concentrated on admiring Colin's cabin. "Oh, this is really gorgeous, Colin. Bernie said your boat was more finished than his. Is that paneling really cherrywood? You have so much more room."

"Hey, you'll give me another complex," Bernie complained. "I can't help it if Colin shows his fancy upbringing. I wouldn't know an antique from an anteater."

"I wouldn't know a computer chip from a potato chip," Colin comforted.

Odd and Essey leaped off Laine's lap and proceeded to charm Midge and Bernie. Bernie bent over so that Essey wouldn't fall from his shoulder where she'd climbed to rub his face with her whiskers.

"We wanted to know if you needed a ride, Laine," Bernie said. "I've got to get Midge home. She hasn't done her homework for my class yet. I wouldn't want to fail my own fiancée."

"Never fail the cook," Midge warned. "It could be fatal to your health."

"I'll take Laine home." Colin lifted Essey off Bernie. "I have to pick up my *Victory*."

"It's still on the dining-room table." Laine smiled into his eyes.

Midge and Bernie exchanged the complacent looks of successful conspirators. "Okay then. We'll see you tomorrow." Bernie waved Midge and himself out.

"Those two would never have made it in the late middle ages," Colin commented, imprisoning Odd and Essey in the hall again so they couldn't follow him. "They couldn't have mounted a successful conspiracy to save their lives."

"I don't know." Laine slipped her hand into his. "It all worked out."

They arrived in time for Laine to compliment Payne on how well her dinner of Cassoulet Ménagère had gone. Payne had thought of the casserole as a main dish that could pick up the leftovers of the week before. Consisting of several meats such as beef, lamb and pork added to vegetables, it made a hearty meal with an interesting variety of tastes. It would appear the next day as Hash Ménagère for lunch. They could offer it for lower prices to the students.

"Payne has already introduced several successful innovations. She's a wonder." Laine praised Payne to Colin, making the girl blush. "I have no idea how I survived without her."

"She doesn't mention the béchamel sauce that I reduced to a goop of paste for the fish last Thursday," Payne admitted. "Nor does she remind me of how I forgot to get the lumps out of the cheese sauce for the croquettes. I don't have Laine's feel for some of those darned sauces, but I'm learning. I have an excellent teacher."

George called from the sink, "I think Miss Laine should start her own school of cookery. She has three good students; Miss Payne, Sam and me. You could give out those medals and ribbons like the French schools do."

"A Cordon Bleu," Payne laughed.

Colin went up to get his statue while Payne and Laine discussed the next day's menu with Sam and George. When he returned, he dropped a kiss on Laine's forehead and promised to see her tomorrow. Payne watched him leave in amazement.

"I never thought I'd ever see Colin show any kind of affection in public. You've done wonders for him, Laine. He looks so different."

"Different?"

"Sort of untight, if you know what I mean," Payne explained.

"I hope you don't mean that knowing me has made Colin come unglued," Laine kidded.

"No." Payne searched for the right words. "I mean he used to seem so tense and strung-up. No, I guess I mean he'd a kind of watchfulness as though he knew a blow was coming at any minute. He never really relaxed. Colin was always good at giving, but he never learned to accept very well. You know what I mean, don't you?"

"I think so. He knows I love him because I told him so. It's relaxing not to have to prove something all the time."

"Oh, Laine, that's wonderful! I told Andy you two were in love. He said he hoped so, but you were both too suspicious of loving and he didn't have much faith in your getting together. I'm so glad he was wrong. I can't wait to tell him."

"Now's your chance," Laine said smilingly. "Here he is to pick you up."

Payne flew over to Andy who waved at Laine as she went into the dining room to consult with the waitresses. Laine had to smile at the affection that lit up the two faces as Payne related her news. Unless she was wrong, those two had a romance of their own going.

April flew by in a cloud of happiness. Colin and Laine spent as much time together as possible. Emilie began to look on Colin as a member of the family as she did Bernie. Often they made a day of it on Sundays with Joy and Frank or Payne and Andy. Plans were made to picnic on Mount Rainier in the summer. They talked of house parties in the summer when Colin opened the Port Townsend house.

Some evenings when Payne took over the restaurant, Colin and Laine just listened to music on the boat, went antique hunting in odd places or talked about each other. Little by little, Laine began to unravel the mystery of the complicated person that was Colin Laird. Her sympathy for the small boy who rattled around a large house, the adolescent who steered his lonely way through high school and the solitary man who could give help so easily but never ask for help himself, bound her closer and closer to the man she loved.

Everyone commented on the changes their love had wrought in them both. Colin's dry sense of humor came to the fore more often. Laine appeared in younger, more becoming styles to please him. Midge began treating him like an older brother. More and more, Laine let her hours of work assume a regular schedule as Payne took a solid hold on the business. When Colin started escorting Laine to church on Sunday mornings, their family and friends happily anticipated the announcement of a wedding date.

"Maybe we could have a double wedding," Bernie suggested to Midge.

"Oh, no!" Midge disagreed emphatically. "That's what everyone tries to do to twins. Double up on everything. A wedding is a woman's own day. I want Laine to be married with all of the trimmings. I don't want to intrude on her special day."

"What if they put it off for a year or so?" Bernie objected.

"They won't. They're both too far gone." Midge was positive. "I'll bet that they set it for the first two weeks of July when the restaurant is closed for vacation. You wait and see."

"What about us?" Bernie was feeling desperate.

"How about the first week in August? That way we'll be married before I start my new job and Joey goes back to school. But don't say anything until Laine sets her date, Bernie. I want Laine's happiness to come first for once."

"August is a long way off," Bernie sighed.

"Is a few months too long to wait for a lifetime of happiness?" Midge kissed him gently.

"Not when you put it that way," Bernie agreed.

Since Joy's due date for the baby was June 15, Laine and Midge planned her shower in May. They refused to limit it to ladies and invited the men, also. It was held on a Sunday, of course, as all their events had to be for ev-eyone to be free.

Joy opened her gifts with such pleasure that even the men lost their discomfort at being guests at a baby shower. Bernie had given them an intercom similar to the one he'd created for Laine.

"You'll want to be able to hear the kid cry if you're downstairs." He was red with embarrassment at Joy's radiant gratitude.

Joy was effusive in her thanks for the tiny baby clothes that the women had given her and admired the silver christening cup Andy had contributed. Colin's gift overwhelmed Joy and Frank. He'd found a small rocking chair of polished oak just right for a child. It was authentic and sturdy, which delighted Frank and Joy.

"He or she will have to grow into it, but everyone should have their own chair." Without hesitation, Colin let Frank wring his hand.

Later, when all of the gifts had been hauled up to the Marshield's apartment and Colin and Laine were alone, they discussed the evening. Laine loved this time with Colin. They talked of Bernie and Midge planning to buy a new house to start their new life. They laughed at Bernie's pride in wearing the sweater Emilie had knitted for him. He was so pleased to have a family. His mother had been an alcoholic and he'd never known his father. Without siblings, Bernie had grown up alone on the streets of New York's slums. He, Emilie, Midge and Joey were looking for the perfect house for the family. Midge had laughed at Bernie's enthusiasm. "Sometimes I think he's marrying me for my mother and son." Bernie had replied, "There's nothing wrong with terrific fringe benefits when you're getting married, is there?"

"I can't understand why they haven't set the date," Laine said, handing Colin a punch cup to dry.

"I think Midge is waiting for you to set your date," Colin answered, taking her arm and steering her into the living room. "Miss Morgan, I have assiduously courted you for the past month and a half. May I now finally ask for your hand in marriage?"

"Yes, Colin."

"Yes, I may ask for your hand or yes, you accept?"

"Yes, to both."

He pulled her to him on the sofa and kissed her soundly. "At last! Can we set a date, like maybe next week?"

"I need a little more time than that. How about the first week in July? The restaurant is closed for vacation, so we can have a two week honeymoon."

The stiffness of his body warned her before she heard his words. "I thought we talked about that. You said you wanted children."

She watched his expression change with bewilderment. "I do. I always have."

"I talked to Beatrice Peterson. She said she'd buy out your half of Maman's for Payne, so that would be taken care of. Payne can get someone to help her. You could phase yourself out in time to give you the freedom to get ready for the wedding. We could take a tour of Europe or do anything you want to do without worrying about the business. You don't want to work after we're married."

"We didn't talk about this specifically." Laine tried to keep a note of panic out of her voice. "I'd no idea you wanted me to give up my work."

"I thought I made it clear that I didn't wany my children to grow up without a mother as I did."

"But your mother didn't work," Laine pointed out.

"I don't want my kids growing up in a shabby apartment on a back alley of a shopping village." Colin's voice had taken on a cutting edge. "I want a woman who's there for me and my children. I don't want them to grow up like..."

"Like I did?" Laine sat up with her cheeks burning. "I should have known. You once said that marriage was someone giving in, and it certainly wasn't going to be you, was it, Colin?"

Chapter Ten

Laine held on to her temper and tried to see his point of view. "I know you don't want what happened to you to happen to our children, Colin. But no one was more loved than Midge and I, and we were raised right here. Do you think Joy and Frank will love their baby less because they work? We can move to a house when the children reach school age, so they can run and play and attend school with neighborhood friends. I could cut down my hours by hiring another cook. I've worked so hard to make a success of the restaurant. How can you ask this of me?"

"You don't need to work, Laine. I have more than enough income for ten families. I can give you all the luxuries you've had to work so hard for all these years. You can be a complete woman with a real home and family."

"Colin, I am a complete woman. My womanliness doesn't depend on where I live. What if we'd buy a house wherever you like and I only worked half days?"

He stood and stalked angrily to the window. "I spent all of my early life loving people who were too busy to love me back. I'm not going to marry a woman who loves her job more than she loves me."

"Colin, I love you more than my life. If you were forced to move somewhere else, I'd gladly give up my business and follow you. But your work is here. You could write your books anywhere if you wanted to quit teaching. Why can't we just try it with me working? If it's too difficult or you feel I'm cheating you of your time, I'll sell the restaurant. What am I supposed to do while you teach every day or work on your books?"

"You'll do what other wives do," he replied tersely. "I want you to think about this seriously, Laine. I want a full-time wife. If you love me, you'll want to make our home the center of our life together. I have to go to a history conference in Portland next week. I'll expect your decision when I get back." He kissed her ardently. "I love you too much to compete with your career. If you decide that I'm asking too much, I'll understand, but I'm not an Andy. I won't be able to hang around on the off chance that you might change your mind, Laine. Please believe that I'm trying to insure the success of our life together."

Two days later Beatrice Peterson contacted Laine and asked to meet her for lunch in the small tearoom of one of the older hotels downtown.

"I know this seems odd," Beatrice greeted Laine. "I always came here for special occasions as a girl and I have a fondness for it. My mother used to buy me glacés on special shopping trips." She looked shrewdly at Laine's withdrawn face but continued on without comment. "I was delighted when Colin called me about the possibility of Maman's being up for sale. Payne's father and I've been extremely pleased with her decision to take a partnership with you. I hope she's been a real addition."

Laine enumerated the contributions Payne had made to the business. She related the innovations and hard work Payne had given to the restaurant. "She has a real future in the field," Laine assured Mrs. Peterson. "She's also terrific with finances and keeping the books. My work load is much lighter because of her."

"Do you honestly believe Payne is capable of running the business alone?" Beatrice watched Laine closely.

"If I make the decision to sell my half of the business," Laine spoke quietly, "I'd see to it that she was ready. The talent is there. Payne merely needs more experience, and she's getting that every day."

"I didn't mean to be presumptuous," Beatrice apologized, frowning. "I understood from Colin that you'd be marrying."

"Yes, but I must decide whether or not I wish to give up my work."

Beatrice sat back as the waitress poured their tea. "It isn't that you're afraid to leave it in Payne's hands?"

"Oh, no! Payne has been a delight. My reason is purely selfish; I love my work. It's hard for me to give it up."

"Then why?" Beatrice asked reasonably, "are you giving it up?"

"Colin doesn't want his wife to work." Laine squeezed a lemon into her tea, avoiding Beatrice's gaze. "He feels a family is a full-time job."

Beatrice's long face broke into an ironic smile. "I can't imagine why he feels that way. His mother didn't work and he was raised virtually as an orphan. We were neighbors of theirs. I didn't work and made a foolish weakling of my son and a frightened coward of my daughter.

The family on the other side of the Lairds had three children. Their mother didn't work, either, but she was a dedicated clubwoman and drinker. One child has now been divorced three times. Another fled to become a beach bum on the West Coast and the third married a teacher. The one who's married to the teacher worked all her adult life to support their four kids and is as happy as a clam."

Laine was startled at the older woman's bald honesty. Beatrice looked at Laine's expression with amusement. "I'm not a total fool, Laine. I've begun to realize that Payne was the best of our investment in children, even though I know it's because we usually ignored her." The flinty gray eyes looked sorrowfully at the long hands clasped in front of her with their expensive diamonds winking in the pink restaurant lighting. "I'm telling you this because I want you to know how proud of Payne we are for having made her own way."

"She's someone to be proud of." Sad, Laine felt a compassion for the older woman. "Children's decisions aren't always the fault of the parent. Both my sister and I were raised to take over the family business. I love it and Midge hates it. Our decisions as adults are ours alone to make. Payne chose one way and Jim another."

"You allowed Midge to make her own decisions. We forced a decision on our son that caused him to choose death."

"My mother felt responsible for my father's death," Laine comforted Beatrice. "The restaurant passes down through the female line in our family. She talked him into staying on. He seemed to love it, but she always felt that he wouldn't have worked himself into a stroke if he hadn't been in a profession that carried so much stress with it. It was years before she could easily enter their old home, and then only because we redecorated it."

"She shouldn't blame herself. It was his decision." Beatrice nodded at Laine's meaningful glance. "You're telling me that I shouldn't blame myself. It was Jim's decision."

"We make a lot of mistakes in the name of loving," Laine agreed.

The gray eyes, so like Payne's, filled, and the tears spilled over onto the diamonds. "I'd like to believe that," Beatrice said brokenly.

Laine put her hand over the shaking ones. "Believe it because it's true."

Lunch was served but both women were too upset to eat. When Beatrice offered her a ride, Laine asked if she could be driven to Midge's house, aware of the fact that Joey would be in school and her mother would be alone.

Emilie had just finished baking when they arrived. Within a few minutes, Beatrice and Laine's mother were seated in the kitchen like old friends. Laine quietly called a taxi and left them to their conversation, knowing that their mother would offer the kind of comfort that Beatrice needed.

She'd only a few days left to decide about the partnership and Colin. Laine threw herself into her work to forget the loneliness of Colin's absence. He'd picked a good time to force her to come to a decision about their relationship. She missed him terribly that week. The kitchen table seemed empty without him waiting there for her to finish work. Laine found she didn't care what she wore when he wasn't there to see her. Deep circles appeared under her eyes from lack of sleep. Beatrice had said that she wouldn't push for a decision, but Laine knew Colin would expect an answer Sunday night when he returned.

It seemed so unjust. Could she make a life without ever working at her chosen profession again? Wouldn't she feel resentment and anger at having thrown away her years of training? Would she take it out on Colin and their children? She couldn't go to Colin unless she could give away the other without regret.

She'd laid her problem before her mother the night before Colin was to come home. Emilie had begun by speaking of her love for Maurice and how she'd lost all interest in the business when he died. Her soft brown eyes suffered for her daughter who had to make a decision she hadn't had to face. She took Laine's hands into hers.

"It isn't what we've worked at for which we are remembered, Madelaine. It is for how much we loved and were loved. Buildings fall to dust, but love is the thing that binds mankind. How much do you love this man, daughter?"

That night Laine made her decision. She loved her work, but she loved Colin more. Without him her days would have no meaning. She'd have to find ways to fill the empty hours when they were apart. His need for this reassurance was greater than hers. She couldn't deny the pain she felt at giving up her career after all the years of struggle, but she now knew that the pain of losing Colin would be more than she could bear.

The next morning she called Beatrice and informed her that she'd sell out her partnership to Payne. It was Sunday and she went to church with a lighter heart, ignoring the sadness lurking around its edges. Colin would be home tonight. She didn't know that Colin, unable to stand the suspense, had called Beatrice Peterson just before his plane left Portland for Seattle. He was astounded by her reaction.

"I'm glad you're pleased, Colin, because frankly I'm not at all happy about this situation. I'm not sure you deserve a girl as fine as Madelaine Morgan. It seems to me that history is repeating itself. You're treating Laine the same way your father treated your mother."

"That's hardly a fair comparison," Colin grated over the phone."

"No? That girl loves you, Colin Laird. She's as talented in her field as you are in yours. Why do the Laird men find it necessary to break their women to their will? What do you have when you've accomplished it?"

There was no reply from Colin's end.

"I personally hope Laine sees the light before she commits herself to you. You don't deserve her. She's worth more than you have to offer." Beatrice hung up on him with a bang.

Payne had listened with horror to Beatrice's dressing down of Colin over the phone. "Mother, I thought you were fond of Colin. How could you hurt him so?"

Beatrice stared at the phone bleakly. "It's because I care for him and for your friend, Laine, that I told him the truth, Payne. That's the best gift I could give them. Let's hope he uses the gift wisely."

Laine was waiting for him at the apartment. The flowers he'd sent her were in a crystal vase on the end table by the sofa. He saw with delight that she was wearing his favorite red dress. The scent of the white roses filled the living room. He couldn't bring himself to speak, but it wasn't necessary because Laine held out her arms to him and he knew her answer from the steady beating of her heart under his cheek. He found himself trembling uncontrollably in her arms. The week had been an eternity. He pulled her to him tightly.

"Did you really believe I wouldn't choose you above anything or anyone?" she whispered in his ear.

His voice was low and husky with the emotion he'd never revealed even as a child. "I've waited so long for someone to say that to me. You don't know how long I've waited for you."

Later, when they could breathe more evenly, they discussed the wedding. "Give me a month or so, Colin," Laine begged. "I have to turn everything over to Payne. The banns have to be posted in our church. It would break mama's heart if I didn't have a wedding dress and all the trimmings. It will be a small wedding with just our friends but still a wedding."

"When?" Colin demanded mournfully into her ear, nibbling the lobe and admiring the pink flush that crossed her cheek.

"July third would be a good date. The restaurant will be closed for two weeks. That will give me a chance to get the apartment ready for Payne. Our friends can enjoy themselves at our wedding because it'll be a holiday the next day. I've always wanted a candlelight service, if you don't mind."

"That's a month and a half," Colin complained.

"If you prefer, I'll marry you tomorrow and let the chips fall where they may." Laine lightly kissed his nose. "It's up to you."

Colin sighed. "You always count on me to do the right thing."

"Yes, I know it's unfair, but you're a gentleman."

"Okay. We can spend our honeymoon in the Port Townsend house. I'll have it opened for cleaning this month. July third it is. I'd better go home before you find you can't get rid of me. You're sure you don't want an engagement ring? You could have a sapphire if you don't like diamonds."

"I want a wide gold band like my mother and grandmother, please." Laine embraced him. "You can give me a sapphire the day we have our first born, if you like."

"That's a promise." He gathered her close for a kiss and Laine realized that it would be wise for them to part now before both of them forgot their good intentions.

May had ended with its usual tenderness and sweet promises making it for Colin difficult to be around Laine without touching her. He watched her patiently instruct Payne about her future duties while continuing to enjoy her friend's company. She appeared to have a bottomless well of caring for everyone around her, and it never seemed to diminish her love for him. When Bernie and Midge announced their August wedding date, Colin found himself rejoicing as much for Bernie as he had for himself. He finally began to realize the true nature of the gift of loving. Under the influence of Laine's love, he found himself expanding and growing much to the delight of those closest to him. A whole new world of caring opened up for Colin.

Joy's baby girl arrived on the scene ten days early. Melinda Marshield weighed in at seven pounds, eight ounces and had her mother's reddish hair and her father's blue eyes. Colin watched contentedly as Laine cuddled the tiny girl in her arms. He was sure she'd forgotten her sacrifice in the fullness of a future that included her own babies and her own home. That is, he was sure until he found her weeping one night after a large party. The guests had presented her with a spoon covered with blue ribbons and a card that read, "To Seattle's own Cordon Bleu." She laughed it off as sentimentality, but he'd read the truth in her eyes.

There were only two more weeks left until her wedding. Laine's wedding dress of white eyelet hung in her bedroom swathed safely in plastic. The fingertip veil that would fall from a daisy wreath was draped beside it. Midge had chosen to wear a pale-yellow eyelet the exact color of the daisy centers.

"I've always loved the idea of a French country wedding." Laine showed Colin the picture of the simple bouquets that she and Midge would carry. "Mother is going to wear lavender batiste over taffeta." She smiled at him and laughed. "I know this isn't exciting for you, but it's very important to a woman. You'll just have to bear with me. It's only two more weeks."

That Monday everything seemed to go wrong for Laine. The roster of reservations was completely filled with many June wedding parties and graduation groups. Then Payne called to say that she had a terrible flu and her doctor absolutely forbade her to come to work for at least a week. She hoped she'd be well enough to help on Saturday. She'd try. With a pathetic sniff, Payne rung off.

On top of everything else, Colin had brought a friend who was visiting him for the week. The dark-haired gentleman with a dashing mustache was introduced as Lou Mountain. He was opening a French restaurant somewhere in the east, and Laine had promised Colin to let him observe Maman's in action. It wasn't his fault he'd chosen the worst possible week to come.

Laine had to explain to Colin that she had to work extra hours because of Payne's illness. He accepted it with surprising ease. He left Lou in the kitchen and promised to drop in when they both had a minute free. She assumed that he also had a terrific work load with the end of the academic year approaching.

In a way Laine was happy to have the kitchen to herself for a short time. She felt that it was a fitting good-bye to her career. She wanted to go out in a blaze of glory, so she planned to serve her special dishes and her favorite creations to the private parties that week. She rose early and went to bed late. She should have been exhausted, but she wanted to give her art one last fling and found that she was exhilirated by competing with herself. The watchful glance of Lou Mountain followed her everywhere as she willingly explained her recipes and serving ideas to him while she worked. They often spoke in French because her French was better than his English. She was surprised at how well George and Sam handled the presence of the little man, but he seemed to know his business and how to stay out of their way.

Laine found that George and Sam were putting in too many extra hours. She tried to shorten them, but both men assured her that they wanted to do this for "old time's sake" as she would be leaving soon.

"We want your last weeks to be especially nice," George stated, his brogue thicker than usual, and Sam emphatically agreed. Nothing Laine could say would change their minds, so she let it go, promising herself that she'd give them a bonus in their paychecks.

Saturday was a particular challenge. A large group called the Seattle School of French Cookery had reserved both of the party rooms that opened into one big one. They'd requested a buffet and had sent a large sum of money as an advance. Laine was determined to give them their money's worth. She was disappointed that Payne was still under the weather and couldn't be there to help, but she, Sam and George had everything under control.

She was having a little trouble with Lou Mountain who kept asking her thousands of questions as she prepared the elaborate meal. He could understand why she chose to serve Fricadelles de Veau and Chicken Sauté Marengo because they both used fresh tomatoes in their sauces. The Boeuf En Daube was always a solid beef dish for a buffet, but he wanted to know why she'd chosen Lobster Américaine as her fish entrée.

Patiently Laine explained as she immersed her julienned celery in ice water to crisp before adding it to minced apple for one of her salads. "It's the best lobster recipe that adapts to American tastes, as you probably know since it was developed in France to please the American palate. The other reason is that I get our lobsters from the east coast and they're closest in taste to the lobster of France. My grandmother's recipes work best with the kind of food they were originally developed to go with." She went on, as she folded the apple into the celery, to warn him about the eggplant dishes that could not come up to the French eggplant and why. He nodded sagely, writing everything down in the small notebook he always carried with him.

When the party room was filled to capacity, Laine and her help used the small door that opened directly into it from the kitchen to set up. Since they were serving a buffet, they drew a curtain in front of the table so that the waitresses could serve the hors d'oeuvres and liquid refreshments while the hot food was being put into its special warming dishes. Laine heard the group ahh over the liver paté in the shape of a suckling pig to let them know it was Paté de Foie de Porc. She'd let Mignon and Betty act as hostesses tonight. Betty was adjusting to her new position well. This kind of meal deserved Laine's full supervision. She felt that the students of French cooking should be served the best of the genre. Besides, she was enjoying herself. After a few finishing touches; some parsely sprigs here and there, and the addition of some apple-in-cinnamon to liven up the veal balls on their platter, she went out the door and signaled Sam to open the curtain so the buffet could begin.

Much to her disappointement, Laine found that Lou Mountain had disappeared. She thought he'd particularly enjoy the treat tower she was creating for the dessert. Of course, the poor man had been there since that morning. He was probably exhausted.

George was busily filling the orders of the customers in the dining room and all was going smoothly. She began arranging an old-fashioned dessert table for her special group. The crystal dishes and silver trays were ready for their occupants. She'd used the color scheme of blue, white and red in honor of the French flag. Several blue vases in strategic places held white and red roses. Sitting in the center of the table on a silver pedestal was an eight-layer Genoise decorated in the theme colors. It was flanked by a color guard of the cake's smaller cousins, the petits fours. Beside the tiny cakes were trays of almond tarts, raisin cakes, ladyfingers, meringues and madeleines rising in different levels to two end towers. One crystal tower supported her special Gâteau Normand with its thin covering of sparkling glacé royale. The other tower consisted of the delicate cream puffs called St. Honoré, filled with rich crème pâtisserie. Situated among the trays and in other tiny places were sugar rosettes in red, white and blue.

As Sam and George removed the dinner table, Laine unwrapped her apron and revealed the new white dress she'd purchsed as part of her trousseau. They carefully rolled the dessert table in behind the closed curtain and she lighted the candles. The table looked like a glittering fairyland. George had put on his tall white chef's hat in honor of the occasion.

"It's so perfect, it's unreal," he whispered. Sam agreed as he took up the silver serving knife and stood on George's other side.

"I had once hoped we'd do many of these," Laine whispered to them. She touched the soft ruffles of her organza dress to make sure they were framing her neck properly. She nodded for George to open the curtain. She'd been requested to join the party for dessert and she'd honor this request.

The party room was dimly lit with candles while the serving area had three bright lights over it so Laine couldn't see her audience clearly. When she did she nearly fainted.

The group standing before her applauding were all her friends. Colin stood at the head of the table. Around it was Midge, Bernie, Payne, Andy, Beatrice and Mr. Peterson. She saw Officer Charlie Dodd with Frank and Joy, who was carrying the baby in her arms. Emilie and Joey were clapping with all their might. Even Professor Rivers, her oldest customer, had been included.

"Oh," Laine laughed. "I'm delighted this was for all of you. I wondered who the School of French Cookery was. I'm so glad I had the pleasure of preparing this last meal for my friends and family."

"Not precisely," the French accent of Lou Mountain came from her left. "I have to admit to you, Miss Morgan, that I was here under false pretenses. My friend, Colin, he told me how you had dreamed of going to my school and could not."

"Good heavens!" Laine suddenly realized that the French equivalent of Lou Mountain was Louis Dumont. He was the famous French chef she'd intended to apprentice under before her father's death.

"During the past week I have given you an oral examination that is more in depth than my students get at school. You thought you were instructing me, and many times you were, young lady." He paused for the polite laugh in the room to subside. "I have observed your practical exams throughout the week. You have shown me that the famous French culinary talents of my people have successfully bloomed across the seas. As the head of Dumont Le Cordon Bleu L'ecole de France, I give you this Grand Diplôme signifying that you are an advanced student of the *grande cuisine*, and I put around your neck this medal on a blue ribbon to signify to the world that you are a true Cordon Bleu." He dropped the ribbon over her head and kissed her on both cheeks. Before the group could reach her he whispered, "You will give me the recipe for that light mustard sauce you used on the apple-celery salad, won't you?"

"Gladly," Laine whispered back.

"Quickly, what was the secret ingredient you used to give it that tang?"

"Sweet-and-sour pickle juice," she replied succinctly.

"Incroyable!" He looked amazed. "American creativity."

Payne was first to hug her. "Colin has been planning this for weeks. He said it was to be your wedding gift!"

Emilie kissed her daughter's cheek. "You see how the Lord rewarded you? You made a decision for love and were given your dream, too."

After the group had finished congratulating her and settled down to devour their sweets, Mignon and Colin led her into the dining room, where some of her best customers were to greet her. Bernie had run a small speaker to the room so that they could hear the ceremony. Again she was overwhelmed with congratulations for her ribbon and her upcoming wedding.

"Colin had me make up a list of our oldest and most valued customers." Midge laughed at Laine's astonished expression. "We invited them two weeks ago. I had to change some people to other nights, but Colin paid for it all."

"You can still call me Lou." Louis Dumont wandered over to her, attacking a large piece of Genoise. "I give that honor to all of my students with the advanced diplomas. I tell you, my dear, you will make my school famous in the Northwest of your country. Believe me, I will be delighted to take credit for teaching I never had to do." He laughed uproariously. "Truthfully, I came to do a favor for my friend, Colin. He kindly included me in his famous book on France and I owed him. I thought I would give you a kind of honorary degree for fun, you understand. At the most, I had hoped you were worthy of a *certificat élémentaire*, but I should have known that Colin would know a true Cordon Bleu when he saw one. He is clever enough to marry you, as well."

Colin joined them, putting his arm around Laine. "I traveled through many countries only to find her in my own homeland."

"Humph," declared Beatrice. "I hope she knows what she's taking on by marrying a Laird. She has a tough life ahead of her."

Colin put his other arm around Beatrice. "She has a mighty champion in case I get out of hand. I bought back our old house next door to yours. Laine and Payne can plan menus to their heart's content when they're not at the restaurant."

Laine looked up at the beloved face with a startled expression. "I don't understand."

"I thought we could live in your apartment until the house is done according to our tastes so we'd both be close to work. My boat is too crowded for two."

"Both be close to work?" Laine couldn't believe her ears.

"You wouldn't want to move into the house yet. The former owner had a penchant for red brocade and paisley that would set anyone's teeth on edge. They painted the kitchen chocolate and beige with mustard trim. It'll take some time to shape it up."

"Oh, wow!" Joy clapped her hands. "Did you hear that, Frank? We get a whole house to do over!"

"We couldn't possibly redecorate without the help of our friends." Colin laughed at Joy's enthusiasm. "Bernie can put intercoms and stereo systems anywhere he wants."

"I've just invented a new system I'm dying to try out." Bernie reached for another raisin cake. "Now these taste like homemade cooking. The other stuff is too fancy to eat."

"Bernie," Midge wailed.

He looked crestfallen. "I was trying to be very good," he apologized.

Laine kissed her future brother-in-law on the cheek. "You are very good, Bernie. We understand. Enjoy!" She grinned at her friend and would never tell him that he was eating one of the more expensive cakes with its imported sultanas, currants and delicate cherries from across the country. Let him enjoy his "homemade" goody.

Laine didn't have a chance to pursue her conversation with Colin because they were both swept away into whirlpools of well-wishers. Eventually the dining room emptied and Louis Dumount took his leave.

"Congratulations again, my lovely Madelaine, on your talent and your love. You have made excellent choices in each field. Madame Beatrice and her husband have kindly invited me to the top of your Space Needle for lunch tomorrow. I will leave from there to the plane. Please visit me when you come to France. I would enjoy having you in my kitchen as I enjoyed being in yours. *Bonne chance,* Mademoiselle Madelaine. *Au revoir.*"

Midge, with everyone's blessings, insisted that Laine and Colin go for a romantic walk. "We'll clean up," she promised. "This is your engagement party. Go walk in the mist and whisper sweet nothings. Only one week until the big day! You two haven't had a moment together all week. Go!"

"Colin." Laine could hardly wait until they were alone in the alley. "Did you mean..."

"I mean." He silenced her with a kiss.

"But I thought this was a wonderful send-off. It was the best ending I could have had before our wedding."

"Not an ending, a beginning. You loved me enough to sacrifice your talent and your work on the altar of my selfishness. I love you enough to trust that you'll never let anything interfere with us. This way I'll always be assured of a great dinner when I come home from the library!"

They walked arm in arm down the familiar street.

From her second floor window, Joy Marshield watched the couple. "Oh, Frank! Aren't they just perfect together? I knew they were kindred hearts. Isn't it wonderful?"

Frank drew his wife into his arms and smiled. "Yes, it is and so are you."

Laine looked deeply into Colin's eyes. "Are you sure? I love you too much to make you unhappy about anything. You've given me so much."

"It was you who taught me that you can't love too much. The well just keeps filling up, Madelaine. The more I love you, the more I want to give. You're addictive. I think I'm falling apart."

She wound her arms around his neck. "I'll put you back together again."

He pulled her to him closely. "You already have, my dear. You already have."

READERS' COMMENTS ON SILHOUETTE ROMANCES:

"The best time of my day is when I put my children to bed at naptime and sit down to read a Silhouette Romance. Keep up the good work."

P.M.*, Allegan, MI

"I am very fond of the quality of your Silhouette Romances. They are so real. I have tried to read some of the other romances, but I always come back to Silhouette."

C.S., Mechanicsburg, PA

"I feel that Silhouette Books offer a wider choice and/or variety than any of the other romance books available."

R.R., Aberdeen, WA

"I have enjoyed reading Silhouette Romances for many years now. They are light and refreshing. You can always put yourself in the main characters' place, feeling alive and beautiful."

J.M.K., San Antonio, TX

"My boyfriend always teases me about Silhouette Books. He asks me, how's my love life and naturally I say terrific, but I tell him that there is always room for a little more romance from Silhouette."

F.N., Ontario, Canada

*names available on request

Silhouette Romance

COMING NEXT MONTH

AFTER THE MUSIC—Diana Palmer
Rock singer Sabina Cane had been warned that Hamilton Thorndon was a formidable man, but nothing could have prepared her for the impact he would have on her life.

FAMILY SECRETS—Ruth Langan
Who was blackmailing Trudy St. Martin? Caine St. Martin and Ivy Murdock joined forces to discover the culprit's identity, and in the process they discovered the secrets of love.

THE HIGHEST TOWER—Ann Hurley
BeeGee was fearless enough to join the Greenings in their work as steeplejacks, but when her heart started falling for Dan Greening she became determined to keep her feet firmly on the ground.

HEART SHIFT—Glenda Sands
Arson…someone had burned down Chris's shop. Chris felt lucky that handsome and imposing Ian West was on the case, until he told her that she was the prime suspect.

THE CATNIP MAN—Barbara Turner
Julia treated life as a serious matter until, aboard a Mississippi riverboat, she met Chad. His infectious good nature chipped away at her reserve and brought laughter and love to her heart.

MINE BY WRITE—Marie Nicole
Professor Kyle McDaniels gladly offered to help Mindy Callaghan with her writing, yet when it came to offering his heart, he was the one who needed a little help.

AVAILABLE NOW:

WRITTEN ON THE WIND
Rita Rainville

GILDING THE LILY
Emilie Richards

KINDRED HEARTS
Lacey Springer

EYE OF THE BEHOLDER
Charlotte Nichols

NOW OR NEVER
Arlene James

CHRISTMAS MASQUERADE
Debbie Macomber